This book is dedicated to
the memory of Frank Lee Johnson, DVM,
renowned veterinarian, family man,
raconteur, historian, and writer.
His wisdom and storytelling skill are missed greatly.

LAB RATS CAN'T SAY NO

A STORY IN THE FUTURE

JEFFREY ALAN JOHN

LUCID BOOKS

Lab Rats Can't Say No
A Story in the Future

"Jeff John puts us in the shoes of reporter John Avila as he digs into the heart of corruption. In a futuristic world where the "Haves" decide just how much the "Have-Nots" get, John's coverage of a local fire upsets his higher-ups. Things get even more complicated when he strikes up a relationship with the boss's daughter. Despite warnings to quit, he can't stop his quest for the truth—even when that truth puts his job, his relationships, his very life at risk. *Lab Rats Can't Say No* takes us on a harrowing odyssey through a future that's scarily believable—one I'm afraid we might wake up in tomorrow. Eerily prescient, it's a story that holds a dark mirror up to the modern world."

—Fredrick Marion,
Freelance writer and founder of www.daytonlit.com

"Jeffrey Alan John takes readers on an exciting and thrilling journey into a futuristic world. I found myself becoming more and more invested with all the characters and the adventurous plot line with every turn of the page. From beginning to end, readers will find themselves on the edge of their seats, wondering what will happen next."

—Rev. Michelle Wilkey, MDiv,
David's United Church of Christ

"Jeffrey John has painted a very accurate picture of a likely future . . . The ending is a pleasant surprise as well, speaking of even farther-ranging technological possibilities for humanity."

—Richard Durrenberg, EdM, BSIT,
Researcher in post-oil civilization

Table of Contents

Introduction

Has the world changed much since the year you were born? Most people, whether they are young or not so young, say they have seen the world change a great deal. But is it really that different, fundamentally?

I arrived on this earth just after the midpoint of the twentieth century. My earliest memories are of my family and the cinder block house my parents built with their own hands on a country road outside a midsize city. I recall our cars, the mixture of old and newer one-story houses that comprised our neighborhood, and airplanes flying overhead. We ate meals, watched television, and went to school or work. In short, the world rolled along then pretty much as it does now.

Many futurists think the path to the world of tomorrow will be different. They lapse into fanciful visions of flying cars, space colonies, and meals that pop out of machines, ready-made and delicious. People may see such wonders centuries from now—my own father, born in 1900, before the invention of the airplane, marveled at the great changes he experienced—but generations now on the planet probably will face a reality far more restrained.

In the foreseeable future, the earth will be forced to support upward of nine billion people. Pessimists expect pestilence and conflict over scarce resources; optimists expect technology to save humanity by expanding those resources. Neither camp seems to recognize how much the seeds of an inhibited future have been sown in the present.

When I was a youth, I had the pleasant experience of spending a great deal of time with a family of means and class; although, in retrospect, I realize the relative moderation of their status. I learned their world was different from mine, not in essentials (and certainly not in bearing) but in accoutrements. They could have things, go places, do things I simply could not. As a guest—a welcomed one, to be sure, but an outlier nevertheless—I was but a visitor from a different society.

Circumstances in the distribution of wealth since then have widened the gap between those who have and those who don't, "the one percent" and the rest of us. That we are coming to a time in the world when only a few will have the wealth and the background to enjoy the diminishing resources of the earth seems inevitable. Applied science will enable enormous gains in lifestyle and health, but only a fortunate few will hold the wealth that will enable these enhancements. And as we already know, with wealth comes power, including control of the channels of communication. Meanwhile, common people will survive as we always have, but like frogs in water heated to a boil, most of us will have become accustomed to our place in society.

Nevertheless, we should be hopeful as we face this challenging future. One need only read the works of the Greek playwrights, the stories of the Bible, or the great plays of Shakespeare to realize the fundamental concepts of human interaction, for good or evil, have not changed. The fantastic technologies merely overlay humanity, like clothing adopted to accommodate changing styles. Human beings will interact as they always have.

This book has smoldered in my mind for years. In its story, I hope to illustrate the coming tensions between humanity and technology. It will be up to us, and the generations to come, to determine the accuracy of my vision.

JAJ
March 2018

Prologue

Da tump . . . da tump . . . da tump . . . My head hurts.
The train's composite wheels hit the old highway's expan-
sion joints in a rhythm that jars my brain. I try to rest by
leaning against the window, but the pane vibrates too much.
Instead, I look outside, where I can see the lead coaches of
the train following the curve of a broad arc in the elevated
road, encircling thousands of twinkling lights that spread
into the distance. I watch as below my window the train
overtakes and passes a slow-moving e-pod, while its disin-
terested occupants turn their vacant stares up toward me.
In the outside lane, a big gas car races past both the e-pod
and the train, its darkened windows pulling a veil between
the car's occupants and the world of common people outside
its sheltering cocoon.

I'm struggling to collect my thoughts. I'm so confused.
I've just left the woman of my dreams lying on the floor,
nearly dead, with a stiff at her feet. She was willing to kill
to save my life. Or maybe she did it to avoid being transformed into something she doesn't want to be. Besides, was
it really murder? And she ordered me to leave, in no uncertain terms. She's probably right—if I had stayed, I would
be the one accused of that homicide, if we're going to call

it that. Without doubt, circuits have been tripped and the ether filled with digital alarms. I know begging me to get out was her way of saving me.

On the other hand, if I don't act, she's surely going to be changed irretrievably. Maybe I can get her out of that bad situation, but I'll have to ignore her pleas. Then, I could get the word out about what I've discovered. I have to realize I'm responsible—I'm probably the only person who's connected all the dots, and if I'm caught, I won't be able to defend myself. No one will believe me.

I can't remember a time when I was so mixed-up.

The train creaks and begins to slow. "Next stop . . . University Place," the electronic voice announces. Below, a block or so away, I spy the shiny new edifice built at the location that has occupied so much of my thinking for the past two years . . . the Borwyn site. I have to admit I've been obsessed, and now that obsession has risen to consume me. It seems like yesterday, when conflict among the powerful and not-so-powerful caught my imagination over a few hectares of earth. The land, the plans for a sparkling new state university building, and the battle over the space combined to draw me into a new world, and the mess I'm in.

I

I remember it all clearly. I was on my way to work one humid, hot morning, when from my window seat on the train, I saw a dark column of smoke rising into the blanched sky like the pillar of cloud that led the Israelites. Pretty big fire just a few blocks away, I thought; I should follow my instincts and check it out. So I did. At the train's next stop, I heard the wail of fire and rescue vehicles' sirens, so when the doors slid open, I was the first person to hop off. I left the station at a run, the noise making it easy to find my way through the maze of city streets toward the conflagration.

I knew I was closing in on the fire when I started to smell the sweet aroma of burning wood. A block or so later, the air was filled with scorched bits of paper drifting down like multicolored snow. I turned another corner and encountered a chaotic scene. About two blocks distant, smoke roiled out of every opening in the top half of an older gray building of about six stories. Here and there, tongues of flame licked into the open air from where windows had blown out, strewing broken glass and rubble all over the street in front of the burning building. Bots and people in various kinds of uniforms scurried everywhere. What a scene: exciting and visual, too. I plugged in my earpiece and lifted my handheld to capture some video.

I had less than 30 seconds recorded when a cop with dark hair tied in a bun under her cap ran up and shoved her hand in front of my lens.

"Whadda ya think yer doin', buster?" she yelled, apparently eager to push her uniformed authority in my face. Just my luck to be confronted by a twentieth-century movie cop. "I'm a content provider," I answered, fumbling for my wallet. "Here's my license. I'm allowed to do this."

She turned her head but barely looked at it. "Not here, yer not. Y'know better than that. No video of us workin'. Get outta here, 'fore I confiscate your device."

Standard Operating Procedure—S.O.P.—I realized as I backed away with an "oops, sorry," mea culpa. I figured I likely could get my hands on a copy of the official report, and together with the few seconds of video I already had saved, it would spice up a nice informative piece. I scanned the view and tried to memorize every scene, every police and fire officer, their actions, everything in front of me. This building wasn't going to be worth a damn when the smoke clears, I thought.

I left the site, taking care not to pass over any yellow tape or get between the cops and the action. With each pace toward my office cubicle, my mind spun with various ways I could write up the facts of the incident and feed it to the Heuristic Analytic Word Generator (the HAWG) we writers hated. When I got to our weary old building, somehow it seemed a lot easier to open the front door and climb the dark, narrow stairs to my second-floor desk at

InfoNet Now. I finally had serious content, an energizing surprise worth my time.

As I expected, I found Bowman already standing at his desk, tapping away at his screen, when I strolled in. He was a dedicated morning person.

"Hear the noise?" I asked. "Know what's going on?"

He pulled an earplug out. "Just some fire," he said, without even looking up. "Big warehouse. The squawk boxes are all over it."

"Yeah? Well, I got video," I crowed. "I jumped off the train and walked up to it. Got a few seconds before a cop chased me off. It's like being a real journalist."

That got Bowman's attention. "You're kidding? Wow! Quick thinking. You can add that to the official reports when they come in."

"Thanks. But I'll do better. I'll post it now and add a few words of description. The management certainly won't mind that, I hope." And that's just what I did. First thing, before the usual rewrite crap, I assembled the notes in a paragraph with lots of descriptive words about the fire, added that to the video, and plugged it into the HAWG. The piece went 24 whole seconds. When the machine regurgitated the story, I slipped the package in with the rest of my copy that day and waited. Until I left that evening and for the next couple days, I waited for a nasty memo from the police, or the city, or the people upstairs, barking about how I should stick to the entertainment stuff that we do best, and leave the real reporting to the officials. But nothing ever came. I figured they must have thought my report innocuous.

A couple weeks later, I was doing a puff piece on a local business that had me shuffling through archived files from some previous months when I came across a standard-form city commission press release video about a meeting. Seems a real estate firm wanted to purchase and raze a warehouse at the edge of the state university campus. The firm's plan was to build a lavish student recreation center with swimming pools, restaurants, and even a swank hotel—all fitting the lifestyle of the typical college student—and lease the facility to the university. But certain elements of the city administration didn't support the transaction. My eyes almost popped out when I saw the address, 112 Borwyn Street. It was the location of the building I had observed in the process of becoming a burned-out hulk.

I scanned more files about that address, temporarily setting aside the business story and the long list of blurbs to disseminate about entertaining people and funny animals that would draw lots of clicks. Little nuggets popped up: a passing mention of verbal jousting between the owner of the building, a Milo Proffitt, and the university lawyer during a hearing; a listing for a date set for an upcoming zoning appeal regarding the property; and an official statement with no author, using the Borwyn Street building as an example of preserving the rights of private property owners. But when I scoured the databases, I couldn't find the files.

"Why isn't this stuff here?" I asked Bowman, who as usual didn't even look up from his screen.

"It's probably a Communist plot or a terrorist attack. Don't bother. Spending hours doing research isn't why they gave you a contract," he said. "Besides, you better not get caught digging like that instead of being creative with the stuff they give us."

Sarcasm oozed out with his words, but he turned serious for a moment. He sat down, spun to face me, and offered some experience-based advice. "But if you're really curious, I bet the county records office is the place to start. Try there first."

Curiosity did annoy me like an itch in the middle of my back. At lunch time a couple days later, I left our building and hiked toward the county government tower several blocks away. The scorching heat of the day radiated up from the pavement and burned my feet through my shoes, while the weighty humidity saturated the atmosphere. The few people on the street gathered in the sparse shade cast by the small trees planted in boxes on the sidewalk, or they protected themselves from the sun by huddling in the meager shade of street-front awnings.

The county building, a large structure of somewhere near ten stories, stood apart from its neighboring towers, separated by a small park with benches, trees, and some wilted shrubs. A pair of doors, which seemed ridiculously small for the size of the tower, served as its entrance. To get to them, I had to climb three flights of concrete steps above street level, then cross a wide pavilion. The armory-like design probably resulted from the city riots of years ago, when a sizeable gathering of angry, half-starved, unemployed people tried to voice their grievances in the relatively open city government offices of the time.

In contrast to the government tower, high-end shops huddled in the shadows of the county center, with open fronts enjoying the cool benefits of their shady location. I found that once I'd climbed the stairs and entered the government center, cool air greeted me there also, and because it was comfortable inside, I didn't mind wandering awhile. Eventually, my tour led me to the records office housed in the basement. Behind its doors, sat a single worker, a small rotund woman with short black hair framing an equally round face dominated by thick, dark eyebrows and puffy red lips. She peered up through black-rimmed, round glasses and said, "Yes?"

"I'm looking for the videos and records of city council and zoning commission meetings from a few months back," I said.

"You can get those online," she sneered.

"No. I'm sorry but they're not there," I replied patiently. "For some reason, those records aren't available online. I was hoping they're here somewhere."

"We got thousands of files. What do you want?" the clerk responded, obviously annoyed. Her name tag identified her as Betty Hinders.

"Betty, could you direct me to the files from three months ago?" I asked, being as polite as I could muster.

"Geez, you people think we've got nothing else to do but chase records. Do you all think we work for you?"

Well, yes, I thought, but I was trying to be nice, and I certainly didn't want to argue about her job responsibilities as a public employee. She groaned, got out of her chair, and said, "It sure would be nice to buy a warm cup of coffee while you're digging through those records, if you know what I mean."

I knew, so I took out my wallet and handed her 20 dollars in paper cash, which she pulled from my fingers as she waddled off toward what turned out to be a back room. "Follow me," she muttered, and we went past rows of rolling metal shelving filled with boxes marked by hand-scrawled dates. The place smelled faintly moist and musty. Eventually we passed into a small room defined by walls of disks.

"Here you are," she said. "They're labeled by group and date. There's the reader. Let me know when you're finished."

Then she shuffled out and left me in the silence of the records. With a little effort, I found the right city council recording from a few months back, pulled the video disk, and popped it into the reader, an old terminal with a screen smudged by uncountable fingers rummaging through city governments past.

Before long, I found the recording of what obviously had been a lively meeting. Council members and the attorneys for the real estate firm and the state university exchanged sometimes heated words regarding the building at 112 Borwyn. Clearly, the university had an intense interest in that property, and apparently others did as well. The attorney only hinted at "agreements," and cited "discussions we've had in the zoning and appeals boards." But at the end of the council agenda item, by a one-vote majority, the council supported building owner, Proffitt. He apparently had influential friends on the council who cited his rights to the rental income it produced. And left unmentioned, of course, were the city's benefits from the tax income derived from the building and its street-level shops and offices, which the city would lose if the property became a state university holding.

The attorney's words piqued my curiosity about the other meetings to which he had referred in his council presentation. I rummaged around on other shelves and found older records for both the zoning board and its appeals group.

It struck me as strange that the files included no video, but I knew analog text files had been created automatically from the audio. I struggled to read the monotone type and lack of formatting, but it was among those files that I found increasingly strident language arguing for and against the firm's takeover of the property. Business people, university administrators, board of trustee members and even a few state officials spoke on behalf of the arrangement between the firm and the institution. The debate led to the zoning board agreeing with the real estate company, a temporary victory for the university planners. On appeal, the building owner and the city won a short-lived victory leading to the council's final vote in Proffitt's favor.

I was sitting at my workstation a few days later when I realized the significance of the timing of this process: a month after the council voted, the building at 112 Borwyn was a smoldering ruin.

II

A few days later, I met the woman who would change the course of my life. Bowman and I and everyone else on the InfoNet Now staff had been invited to the company's annual dinner bash, a big deal where the upper echelon poured the company propaganda on the audience like pancake syrup. We were required to attend, but they made it worthwhile by providing lots of real shrimp as big as your middle finger, various breads and cheeses, good wine, and other treats designed to get us mellow before the speeches. We anticipated a main event that featured a meal of authentic chicken and fresh vegetables while the executives pranced on the showcase floor in the middle of the room, showing us 3-D charts and graphs of InfoNet Now successes.

I did get pretty mellow before the presentations began, distracted to the point of not caring about the upcoming facts and figures. Finally, I spotted someone else I knew: our department's administrative assistant. Tall, slender, and handsome, with long, wavy brown hair and olive skin tones, Lucy Noble stood a head above the group of women who gathered around her. Her hazel eyes met mine, and she beckoned me over with a curled finger.

"There's someone here I want you to meet," Lucy said as she guided me into the circle. "Indy Lexar, this is one of our content providers, John Avila."

"Hi," the woman said as Lucy backed away. Apparently, I was now flying solo, with an attractive young woman who had a last name I recognized as important in the company.

"Indy. That's an unusual name. Short for Indianapolis?" That was the best I could think to say. My muddled brain couldn't come up with anything more clever, and I didn't want to make any embarrassing accusations about her surname.

"Short for Indira," she replied, not acknowledging my feeble attempt at humor. "My mother was from a family that emigrated from India. But that's about as much as I know about her side of my family. She passed away when I was quite young. Since she died, my father has seen to my care."

Our conversation moved along quite nicely once I got over my state of nervousness. Indy's alluring deep-brown eyes paired with her shy-but-happy little smile intoxicated me far more than the wine, and we became our own little island amid a rolling wave of party participants. Indy seemed fascinated with my work, and we were so preoccupied with each other that eventually Bowman had to come over and intervene, dragging me back to reality by grabbing my right arm and trying to pull me away. "It's time to sit down for dinner," he whispered loudly in my ear. Surprisingly, Indy became a bit rattled when Bowman intruded on our tiny space.

"Do you want to sit with us?" I asked, trying to continue her enchanting company and conversation. But her bright smile had turned off. Her light flickered like a dying candle.

She leaned over and spoke very softly into my left ear. "I'm expected at another table, but I'd enjoy spending more time with you. Here, I'm sending you my number. Contact me, okay?"

I was floating and didn't even think to ask how she knew my contact information until I finally joined Bowman at our table, set with real china and shiny utensils. His face was filled with a mischievous grin.

"So what's up with you?" I asked. "You almost ruined a wonderful thing I had going."

"I saw you talking with that gorgeous woman. You do know who she is, don't you?"

"Uh, no. Not really. I recognized her last name. Lexar. Is she part of the owner's family? She said her name's Indy. We were just enjoying a pleasant, innocent conversation. What's the harm in that?"

"Be careful. She's the boss's daughter. Not some assistant manager in the next office. The grand pooh-bah. Paul Lexar, the big cheese. He doesn't mix with us grunts. I'm surprised his daughter does."

"Well, I'll find out, 'cause I have her number," I said, rather smugly. "She gave it to me. We'll see if she's willing to mingle with the worker drones."

III

The next day, I contacted Indy using the number she had given me. She chided me mildly (though I detected a definite smile in her voice) for waiting so long to contact her—it was only around noon—and we agreed to meet after work at a coffee shop near my office.

It was a drizzly day, and the streets were filled with people fleeing the raindrops when I entered the coffee shop. Inside, the Venetian blinds had been drawn, and the walls were painted a dark color, so my eyes took a moment to adjust. Then, I saw her sitting in a corner at the back of the room.

"You're a couple minutes late," she teased, but she was smiling, and I knew my minor tardiness hadn't spoiled our coffee date.

"I try to be fashionable," I replied. We fell into an easy exchange, rolling in turn from our times through the pace of life, to our typical daily activities, and then to sports. She described her family as extremely competitive. Her father had been a star athlete in college, and then he played professional football briefly, back when the game was big, before it faded. She, on the other hand, enjoyed tennis. Being a fair player myself, I had hardly begun to describe my backhand when she challenged me to a match. The catch was, it would be at her home.

"You have a court nearby?" I asked.

"In my backyard. I guess Father decided years ago that we needed a court more than we needed a lawn. So all we need to do is walk out the back door to play."

The place was a bit distant and isolated in a suburb inaccessible to public transit. When I confessed to lacking my own wheels, or having a driving license, Indy laughed. "I'll be glad to come and get you," she said. "I have an e-pod and a license, too. I'll pick you up at ten on Saturday. You do have a racket, don't you?"

Assured that I had the proper gear, she showed up at the appointed time in a shiny white recent-model Alfa Romeo e-pod. I must have looked impressed, because as the car accelerated, smooth and silent, Indy grinned and sat back in her plush leather seat facing me. "Neat, isn't it?" she asked. "We have a couple of these and a gas car, too. Now that thing *goes!*"

I didn't know what to say. Neither I nor anyone I knew before this experience owned any kind of vehicle. Merely riding nonstop at the same pace and level as other cars on the road fascinated me. Then, the e-pod turned in to Indy's suburban neighborhood, with emerald mowed lawns surrounding all the houses. We pulled into a driveway, where the car door popped up and Indy slid out, spreading her arms as if to embrace the view of her large, two-story house. Its old-English style exuded aristocracy: brick tastefully shared the wall space with cream-color stucco, accented with dark wood. Shutters that looked authentic flanked tall windows segmented by many small diamond-shaped panes. A curving path led from the e-pod in one direction through orderly, colorful gardens to a massive, ornate oak front door framed by stone arches. In the other direction, the path ended at a smaller door in an annex attached to a garage. Four enormous roll-up doors, painted to match the stucco, hinted at a fleet of vehicles inside.

"Here it is. Grab your racket," Indy said. "We'll go straight to the courts in back. No need to cause a commotion inside." So we passed around the side of the house and encountered a backyard that consisted of a terrace with some metal chairs and tables, the kind with an umbrella pole in the middle. But the back property was mostly a full-size tennis court with a striped, carefully maintained clay surface. I tried to hide how impressed I was.

"Nice, isn't it?" Indy asked. "The whole thing was my birthday gift some years ago."

Soon, I realized she used it a lot. We stretched, warmed up with a few shots and serves—every one of hers dropped perfectly inside the service box—and then we agreed to keep score. I had thought I was pretty good at tennis—even took a few lessons—but Indy surprised me. Although she wasn't particularly athletic, she would glide to the exact spot and return my shots with effect. I'd hit a ground stroke with all the force I could muster, and she'd return it with equal power. She knew when to volley, dropping deadened shots at the net in front of me or smashing them past me. I'd try to hit it over her, and she'd take a careful step or two back to reach the ball and fling it to some remote corner. By the time we had played two sets, Indy's game had humbled me. I was able to count but a few winning games.

At least she didn't make a big deal out of it. When she said, "Let's take a break," I feared she would send me home with contempt for my lack of skill on the courts, but instead she volunteered that we must both be tired and hungry. I followed her into the house, through a large traditional kitchen to a dining room table covered by a tablecloth, where we found glasses full of ice water, sandwiches stuffed with what looked like real meat, and fresh fruit on plates. Exquisite dark woodwork surrounded us and looked authentic.

"Who did this food?" I asked. "How did they know we were ready?"

"Oh, Ana Maria makes it," Indy replied. "She's been my nanny and housekeeper for so long she knows when I'm done on the court. I think she can see it in my game."

I merely nodded as I dug into a sandwich of real ham and cheese.

"Ana Maria's been my guardian almost since my mother died," Indy continued. "She's family. My father's rarely here anymore. He shows up in the evening. I assume he sleeps here, and then he takes off again early."

"You never see him? Talk with him?" I asked after I had gulped down an impolite-sized bite of sandwich.

"When I do see him, it's like he's giving me orders for the day."

"So you don't get along well?"

"'Get along' is a good way to put it," she said. "It's like he's here, but he's not. Work is everything to him."

Despite my unrefined manners, Indy seemed to like my company. We shared an easy back-and-forth about her work in InfoNet Now—she was a payroll auditor of some kind, so she knew how much everyone was paid. We talked about the cost of things and about the furnishings of the house in which we sat. When we rose from the table, Indy pointed out the impeccable dark-oak flooring, spoiled, she said with a chuckle, by a few scratches imparted when an old boyfriend dragged an iron statue across the floor. Then, she ushered me to an adjacent entertainment room where we watched some funny videos on her high-performance 3-D system. It was dazzling.

Apparently, my efforts to show that I could be couth met her standards. "You want to play tennis again?" she asked later that evening as we whirred home in her Alfa e-pod. "We can go to the club next weekend. But you'd have to wear whites. The club's very traditional."

"I can do that," I said, while thinking where I could get white tennis clothes. "I'd love it."

* * *

The club that weekend fascinated me. The many big gas cars that filled the parking lot warned me that something would be different at this place, and I was right. My tennis that day wasn't so good—grass courts were new experiences for me—but the players were gracious. And I noted that all were my age or younger. There were a few people nearby who looked somewhat more senior, but they sat in the shade and watched. None of them played, or even got up to move around much for that matter.

At one point, a ball bounded off my racket toward a pod of older people sitting at a café table. The ball glanced off the feet of a gentleman, who twitched, belatedly it seemed, and then reached over very stiffly, as if he were propelled like one of those stop-motion creatures in classic science-fiction films. He wasn't able to reach the ball, but all the members of the little group smiled nicely and nodded as I snatched up the errant shot.

I guess I behaved appropriately that day, too, because Indy contacted me the next morning, and we began seeing each other often. She would text me a note, and we'd meet in a pleasant little neighborhood tavern after work. Unlike most of us, she never talked about her job within InfoNet Now, a vast conglomerate with fingers in information and data processing, entertainment, real estate, and legal and financial consulting. Indy didn't seem to have a management-level position. A smallish, black-haired beauty, she would show up in a casual print blouse and plain skirt or slacks, flat shoes, and perhaps a simple necklace. She liked earrings, especially dangly ones, but not rings, which she rarely wore. "I have a couple diamonds Father gave me," she once said, "but I don't wear them. They're ostentatious."

Indy did seem to know important people, or at least people of wealth. We dined frequently with her friends at restaurants I could barely pronounce, much less afford, but mostly we were treated as guests. Over time, I began to realize how comfortable she and her lifestyle made me feel. I hoped we had a relationship that could turn into something.

IV

I wasn't sure Indy felt the same way about me as I did about her. As we grew to know more about each other, she seemed to enjoy pointing out the human traits that made us different. One incident in particular provided a good example. In an attempt to show my own level of material resources, I had invited Indy to play tennis at courts my apartment complex proudly advertised as one of the many perks of living there. We found them to be old and rather worn, with cracks in the hard surface widened by weeds here and there, and a tired net sagging and torn. But we were able to tighten it and play a few games, judiciously avoiding the splits in the concrete. We had just about finished a set when angry clouds the color of gun metal threatened from the west and drove us off the courts. Big raindrops splattered around us just as we reached the doors to my place.

I wasn't ashamed of my apartment. I had cleaned it up in anticipation of this visit, and being an employed single person, I was able to afford a place more comfortable than the living spaces of most of the general population. I had a nice-size bedroom, a functional bathroom, and a living room with windows that offered the potential of a nice view from my third-story location, even if the world outside the window didn't provide much worth seeing. The floor plan featured room for a dining table, which I filled with a desk, and a space that at one time had been a large kitchen when those were popular. I used it for a utility room, with the requisite microwave, a little refrigerator, some storage space, and a washer-dryer unit. I even set up a little table and chair where I could enjoy the take-out meals that I brought home, or the occasional substances delivered by the grocery drone. I had a couch, a comfortable chair for reading, and a coffee table that seemed to collect junk.

Indy and I opened the door to my apartment as a roll of thunder shook the building. Although it was midday, I had to turn on lights; the sky had darkened to a greenish-midnight hue, and in a few moments, hard wind lashed rain against my living room windows, which faced the storm's intensity. As I gathered glasses full of cold water, Indy showed some discomfort.

"Come here and stay with me," she said as she settled onto my couch. "Storms scare me."

"They fascinate me," I replied. "Look at the power of nature. And we haven't yet figured out a way to change it. Lord knows we've tried. Humans have just about wrecked the climate."

I didn't sit with her. Instead, I stood near the windows, watching the wind bend the few little trees by my building nearly sideways. Rain swept down in sheets. Lamps on the sidewalks around my apartment building lit up and cast pitiful little pools of illumination around each pole.

"I have to admit this one's pretty nasty," I said.

"Enough," Indy said. "Come here."

So I abandoned my observation, and at her request, I fidgeted with my handheld's connection to my old monitor. It didn't project a holographic image like modern devices, but it provided a nice view of some old videos that we could access, which I admit I interrupted occasionally to check the progress of the tempest. Storm warnings were being issued everywhere.

Indy and I paid far more attention to each other than we did to the images dancing on the screen. Then a message interrupted us. Bowman's face filled the screen.

"Hey, John, sorry to bother you. Answer, would you? Something's happening."

I picked up my handheld and turned it so Bowman wouldn't see Indy. "What's up?"

"A tornado's blown through one of the far burbs. Damage, but nobody knows how much yet. Franco wants somebody out there. He thinks it will draw lots of eyeballs. Great drama. Human interest." He paused before he continued, "I know you like to do that kind of reporter stuff. I sure don't want to. Can you go?"

Bowman was right. This sounded like the kind of challenge that stirred my blood. "Sure. Where is it?" I blurted, without thinking of my current circumstances with Indy.

"It's on Route 42 south of Ehrling. You'll have to take a train way out, then get a rideshare. You should be able to find the storm damage easy enough. Franco says he wants lots of images. Use your video drone. And get close-ups. See if you can get people crying. You know, emotion. I'll be back in the office to get your content and put it into the HAWG. Get going. Good luck."

"I'm on it," I said as we disconnected.

Indy looked at me with eyes wide open and mouth agape. "How can you get so excited about exploiting those victims?" she sputtered. "That's inhuman!"

"I'm a content provider. I'm paid to get stuff to push out to the InfoNet Now audience. Believe me, it's usually not so dramatic. But I hate to say it, Franco's right. It will get lots of attention."

"Why? What makes people want to see other people suffer?"

"You work for the company, too. It's what we sell. That's the way it is." I couldn't think of a better explanation at the time, because I was trying to think about where to find my recorder and drone.

"Sorry, but I've got to go now," I said. "I've got to get a train."

"I guess I never realized this end of the company's business," Indy replied. "Now I'm curious. Let me go with you. I've got my e-pod here. I'll take you. I won't get in the way."

I couldn't argue with that logic. It would make things so much easier. So we climbed into Indy's car as the gist of the storm was passing and clouds were beginning to lift. Her machine came to life with a barely perceptible whine, then backed out and sped out of the city, following directions I had plugged into it, through suburbs and then a countryside of solar panels, windmills, and giant hydroponic farm barns. Indy filled the time with questions about what I would do and what to expect.

"What will we see?" she asked naively.

"Don't know. Won't know till we get there," I replied. "In my experience, the one thing I notice is the quiet. Nobody says anything. There's nothing to say really."

"Won't the rescue people be there? Why can't you get the information from them?"

"It's not their job to be content providers. I wouldn't trust what they had to say anyway. Besides, they'll be busy."

"Will you help dig people out?"

"That's not my job."

"Will there be dead people?"

"Don't know. Maybe, if it was a big tornado. Hope not."

After about an hour of riding, we encountered litter on the roadway, then large branches from trees. Without an address to guide us, Indy took control of the e-pod. We followed an ever-increasing trail of debris until we spied a small community in the distance.

We had just passed a sign proudly proclaiming "EHRLING, HOME OF THE GIRLS' SOCCER STATE CHAMPIONSHIP" dated some 20 years previous, when we encountered the roofless remains of someone's home. The roof lay jumbled about 200 yards away in a field littered with torn insulation, shattered solar panels, and large pieces of broken wood-like material. Down the road, the next structure hardly befitted the name. A few interior walls of what had been a house stood exposed to the drizzle in the failing light of evening. Near the road, a man in muddy jeans and an overweight woman in shorts waved at us.

"You from the rescue people?" the man said.

I leaned over Indy to answer. "Nope. I'm media. Haven't you seen any emergency personnel yet?"

"No. And I don't have any money to give them when they do show up," the man responded.

Indy pulled over, then we got out. The situation was just like I had described it. Silence hung over the area like an invisible fog. We approached the couple, who were both dripping wet, and while I unfolded my little video drone, I asked if they had seen any other people. Indy began to speak quietly with the woman. The man, a tall, bald fellow bleeding slightly from a cut on his head, said his neighbor had come over briefly to check on the welfare of the couple. She had gone back to help her husband, who had hurt his leg.

I launched my drone and turned to tell Indy that I would move on to those people, but she was walking toward her e-pod. "I'll be back," she said as the door closed. I thought perhaps the scene had been a little too harsh for her.

I thanked the man and woman, got a few lines of identification from each, and invited them to join me as I searched for their neighbors. They declined, so I sloshed alone through the rubble, stepping carefully to avoid the many exposed nails protruding from the shattered building material lying around, while at the same time, I used my handheld to direct the drone into slow circles around the area. The next house stood about 300 feet distant, looking in better shape than the first one we had encountered.

I walked through the opening that had once been the front door and found that looks can be deceiving. In the back of the interior, a woman stood over a man sitting in a chair with big blue cushions. It looked like a comfortable room, except that the sky was visible above them; there was no ceiling. Most of the wall behind them, like the ceiling above, had blown away.

"Hi. Are you okay in here?" I asked, but then I realized how stupid that must have sounded.

The ruins of their home looked like they had been drawn from photographs of a war. "Are you from the emergency management agency?" the man asked very quietly.

I explained that I was a content provider and offered condolences. I gathered names and addresses—Treyl Manuel, 7564 State Route 42, his wife, Eliana, and their son, Tom. It was a strained conversation. Mrs. Manuel, red-eyed and obviously tired, could only speak in a shaky voice as she and her husband described the storm. I turned on my handheld's audio recorder.

"He was standing right by the window," Mrs. Manuel said of her husband. "If he had stayed there another minute, I . . ." She turned away, gazing at the opening that once had been a back wall of her home, as if she contemplated how much worse it could have been. I wished I was recording video.

"We just got down the steps, about halfway to the basement," Manuel noted, "when she let go." He sighed and added, "We just moved here in July."

The Manuels, with Mr. Manuel limping noticeably, then took me to other parts of their home, pointing out the damage. Much destruction was obvious—the back half of the house lay in pieces in the fields beyond their yard. Manuel explained some odd results of the storm, showing chunks of glass embedded in the living room walls and some furniture that had survived, miraculously undamaged. Under a throw rug, the storm had deposited a neat swirl of dirt and glass where the door had been blown away. I lifted my handheld to capture video. Manuel didn't seem to mind.

He pointed to the gaping hole in the living room ceiling, the area most seriously damaged in the house. The interior below the missing structure appeared intact, though a scene of confusion now, with family members sifting and moving debris under a slight drizzle. Manuel said he hoped his home would be restored, but until then, he and his wife would stay with their son, Tom, or "Maybe the government will provide a place," he ventured.

We returned to the front entryway, where Mrs. Manuel was now sitting on a cardboard box, softly weeping. With the video recording the scene, I mentioned what looked to me to be an antique collection, and she said although some pieces had been spared, several tens of thousands of dollars' worth of items appeared to have been lost. She pointed in explanation to wet furniture and broken vases now piled in the living room.

"In a sense we're lucky," Mrs. Manuel said as she turned toward me. "We're just thankful none of us got hurt bad. 'Cept Treyl's leg. It's pretty bad banged up."

I left the Manuels through the hole in their back wall. I scanned the outside with my handheld, capturing video of the view. It made an interesting shot, with pieces of housing scattered in the fields off into the distant gathering darkness. At my command the drone landed at my feet, and as I folded it, I thought it probably held even more interesting video.

I circled the house to find that Indy had returned. She was distributing hot coffee, sandwiches with real ham and cheese, and fruit to the victims of the storm. "That's awfully nice of you," I said, "but the government crews will be here any minute to take care of these folks. It's not your responsibility."

"Oh, yes it is. Obviously, you don't care about them. I do," she replied. Just then, a large drone dropped out of the sky, hauling a load of at least a dozen pizzas. Indy turned toward the gathered storm victims who had been attracted by the sound and the lights. "Help yourselves!" she yelled. "We'll get more if you need it!" I saw Mrs. Manuel and her son pull off the last couple boxes before the drone lifted off and buzzed away.

"I offered my condolences," I said. "But it's not my job to be a lunch wagon. There are other people paid to do that." Those officials were, in fact, arriving just at that time. Search drones passed overhead, lighting the area and broadcasting assuring words that help had arrived.

"It's getting time for us to get out of here," I said to Indy. "Could I use the power in your car to beam my content back to the office?" She rolled her eyes and gave me a look of disgust, but the door popped open in her e-pod. I slipped in and punched up the codes with no trouble.

On the way home, Indy broke a long silence. "Okay, now that I've seen it, I still don't get it. It's really exploiting those poor people to extract information. To do it, you have absolutely no empathy. It's like you don't have any human feelings."

No one had ever pressed me about my work like that. I didn't know what to say.

"I guess I have to shut down my emotions. I have to record content. If I get personally involved, I might avoid some things or miss something that might make a great story. Like that woman tonight in her wrecked home. That was real."

"What a job. I can't believe our company uses people like that."

"Oh, come on. InfoNet Now sells advertising. You need an audience to sell. I provide the audience. Face it, getting people to show their feelings entertains that audience. It's business.

"By the way, how could you afford that food you got those folks? It must have cost a fortune. Are you going to hit up the company for it?"

"Of course not. That was pocket change. I guess I was trying to counteract the company's lack of humanity. It's just another way we're losing our—" my handheld interrupted Indy at mid-breath.

"Pick up! Pick up! Are you there?" Bowman's excited voice announced.

"Yeah, what's up?" I replied as I turned on the video in the e-pod. His image at the other end grinned from ear to ear.

"That content you uploaded was great! Really gripping! Dramatic! It's already up and getting tons of clicks. So many eyeballs!"

∨

Indy wasn't put off by the storm incident. On the contrary, it seemed to cement our relationship. She had seen the professional side of my personality and seemed to tolerate it. I got a chance to see her warm heart and genuine charity toward other human beings. Perhaps it was those contradictions that gelled our relationship as the days flew past. We would stroll hand-in-hand through the parks, and in time, the leaves there changed to gold and red hues, and the air took on a biting chill. We turned to activities mostly indoors, plays and concerts, but one week, Indy offered a new experience.

"How would you like to visit some friends in the country and go ice-skating?" she asked. "We've been invited for that and dinner."

How could I disagree, I thought, and that weekend we climbed into a big gas Tesla sent to pick us up, greeted another couple already aboard, and rumbled off into the night. The machine took us on a curvy road through a snowy countryside lit by a full moon. We leaned into corners and grew weightless in our seats as we rose and fell over hills and dips in the road.

After a ride of many miles, the car passed through a gate leading to a long, wooded lane punctuated by a lighted estate. When our vehicle had rolled to a stop, the doors popped open, and we were greeted by a number of bundled people.

"Hi, Chase," Indy said. "That was quite a ride. John, this is Chase Cameron, our evening's host. He put this party together." I greeted a tall, slim young fellow, who assembled the group and led us to the ice rink—in reality, a swimming pool left filled to about three feet from the top and frozen. He distributed skates, and we all hopped onto the ice, showing skating talents that varied from those twirling and slashing—their flashing blades spreading twinkling ice—to lesser skaters, such as myself, who groped along the edge with occasional forays into the swirling mass of moving people.

Eventually, skaters began to tire and climb off the ice. We were warming ourselves with hot chocolate when Chase stood up. "Those who want can follow me into the library. We've got a fire in there. Or you can stay out here and skate. Dinner will be ready in a few minutes."

Indy and I accepted his invitation. We followed him through a thick wood door in a big round structure made of stone and into a circular room that must have been designed by a librarian. Hundreds of books filled shelves that rose three stories from floor to ceiling, their dominance broken only by a large fireplace with a crackling fire and a small bar. Overstuffed sofas surrounded a round coffee table of weathered wood in the room's center.

"Join me in something to warm you up?" Chase asked from behind the bar.

"Sure, as long as it will warm me up," I replied, as I took a little glass filled with something bright cerulean and aromatic. I eased myself into a comfortable coffee-colored leather chair.

"You guys notice that we've got real chestnuts roasting in the fire," Chase announced. "You don't get those at many places anymore."

We all laughed, and of course scratched out a few rough verses of the old song. Chase plopped down next to me.

"This is pretty amazing," I said. "Was this always the library of the estate?"

"No, this was a grain elevator, believe it or not," he replied. "When I went to law school, my family decided I needed a place to study. How can you beat this, right?"

"So you're a lawyer now, huh? How did you get to know Indy?"

"Through her father," Chase said. "He hired me. No, actually, to be more accurate, his firm hired my firm."

"For anything interesting?" I asked, trying to make polite conversation.

"Well, yeah, I'm part of a legal team that's suing the city. It's been surprisingly difficult. There's this guy who apparently has friends with juice in city council. He and the city just won't listen to reason. Or money.

"Ironically, the place was a big warehouse with some shops and offices, but it burned down. So now we're fighting over rubble. Pity. A woman died in that fire. A janitor."

I tried to keep from leaning forward, my eyes wide open, but I had to keep a poker face. "I think I heard about that. Isn't it the state university that's going to court?" I asked. "Why are you involved? Why should InfoNet Now care?"

"Indy's father is on the university board of trustees," Chase said. "But he doesn't get involved at my level. We correspond about the case a little, but mostly he keeps out of it."

I knew enough to shut up at that. Besides, Chase rose at that point and ushered us out of his library and to the dining room of the estate. A few steps through the crunchy snow took us into a large white mansion and a marvelous buffet of real beef, fresh, multicolored vegetables, and chunks of real dairy cheese. How did I get so lucky, I thought.

Later that evening, sitting with Indy in the comfort of her home's electronic playroom, I could see in her eyes an unusually intense, almost desperate, longing toward me. Coming from a person usually so much in control, it was almost scary, as she nestled next to me.

"I don't think we can get much closer on this sofa," I said with a chuckle.

"Wanna bet?" Indy whispered.

Then I heard a rustling sound and looked up to see a leg in pajama pants and a slipper creep past the doorway and jerk out of sight.

"Who was that?" I whispered, but I knew.

Indy sat up quickly. "That was father," she said. "I don't think he even saw us. He doesn't move very well anymore. I guess the injuries caught up with him.

"He doesn't care what I'm doing anyway. I'll try to talk to him in the morning and see if he was spying on us."

I found out the next day that she did talk with him shortly after, and I guess it wasn't very pleasant. When Indy and I met for lunch, she wore a look of discomfort.

"My father knocked on my bedroom door this morning and said he didn't like me seeing you," she said. "He didn't even bother to open the door."

"What? Uh, why?" was all I could utter. "Didn't he like us together on the couch?"

"I don't even think he saw us. He just said you're too nosy."

"About what?" I asked. "What are you—we—going to do now?"

"Nothing," Indy replied. "I'm going to ignore him. He doesn't run my life. Just be cool. We won't go to the house for a while."

But I wasn't in a mood to "be cool." I was starting to get curious.

VI

I stood at my workstation a couple days later when Lucy Noble's voice surprised me with an audio-only call. Though not necessarily strange, it did strike me as unusual. Until she spoke up.

"The bosth wanth to sthee you," she said. I knew it was Lucy, but she sounded as though she were speaking with a mouth full of cotton.

"What's up?" I asked.

"Don't know. He justh wanth to sthee you."

"Geesh, Lucy, did you have some dental work done or something?" I pursued in my best journalistic tone. No answer.

When I got to her desk, I found out. The left side of Lucy's usually thin face, from her chin to below her left eye, glowed in shades of black, fading to purple-red-and-yellow hues displayed on a puffed-out pallet. I stepped back, stunned by her painful-looking mask.

"Whoa! What happened to you?" was all I could blurt out.

She looked down at the floor to avoid my exploring eyes. "My boyfriend."

"How?"

"He thought I wath methin' around. Beat on me like a cheap drum. I couldn't sthop him." She paused, choking back tears. "Look what he did to me," she whispered. "I got bruitheth all over."

"Damn," I said. "Bad rhythm and blues. Anything I can do?" But I knew, in asking, that thankfully I was out of that particular loop. Didn't know anything about domestic violence, and I really didn't want to get involved in that kind of dispute. "Maybe a good shot of whiskey will help kill the pain." I was trying to be funny, but I knew I wasn't.

Yet Lucy smiled a little. "Just go in. Misther Franco is waiting for you."

Our department's managing director, Adolpho Franco, had a penchant for throwing wrenches into our projects and then bragging about results after we worker bees fixed each problem. He demanded that our workspaces be clean, "like a banker's desk," but at the same time he expected that we produce a steady flow of products that generated clicks, worthwhile or not. "Eyeballs mean audience, which means income" was his motto.

I wasn't in his office much, because he didn't often deal with the rank and file. I squinted when I walked in, because his desk was positioned in front of a massive window. The reflection of light on his highly polished desktop blinded me. He could sit and watch the weather, I thought, although the view that day was a featureless white sky.

"I see you've been generating copy about that fire on Borwyn Street a few weeks ago," he announced immediately. A rather large man, he dressed neatly and formally with long, solid-color ties. Big, tortoise-shell glasses emphasized his roundish face, which was crowned by an old-fashioned, military-style flattop. With his deep voice, he filled the space around him. I noticed there wasn't a chair, sofa, or bench in the room that would have allowed me to sit down.

"I thought it was news," I said. "And now there's more. I hear somebody died in the fire. Nobody seems to know that. I'm digging up the facts now."

"Don't bother. You think you're some kind of cool reporter or something?" Franco boomed. Clearly, he was annoyed. "Forget it. That stuff'll come to light if it's import-ant. It isn't. Nobody cares about it. You're not being helpful."

Stubbornly, and in hindsight foolishly, I pushed on. "But that's it exactly. It *is* important. People need to know about it, but nobody seems to want that information out."

"InfoNet has better things for you to do," Franco said with irritation. "To get you busy doing something worth-while, I've got a project for you." He tossed a flash drive at me and slid some papers across his desk. "This company is buying some ads from us, but in return they expect some copy out in the world. Make this interesting and post it." He leveled his gaze, then said, "And stay off the fire stuff."

"How about if I do it on my own time? I just want to report the truth."

"No!"

I turned and shuffled out, tapping Lucy's desk as I passed. "Let me know if there's anything I can do," I whis-pered. When I got to my workspace, I opened the flash drive and found my task was to enlighten the world about a new road-paving system. I had in front of me what seemed like hundreds of statistics about road-building ingredients, proper crushed stone, and other factors like costs per mile. I had hours of construction video, some still images, and lots of talking heads delighted to profess their faith in this new paving method.

It took a couple weeks to assemble several marketing packages, and I did a good job, if I do say so myself. The content used all kinds of media to explain the wonders of this less-than-exciting new road-paving system: our animation people helped me create 3-D videos, we had social media blurbs, and I even wrote some copy for print media. But through the whole project, always the warehouse fire flickered in the back of my mind. I pondered how to get at the unreported facts and devised strategies to avoid further problems with Franco.

As I neared wrapping up the road-building packages, I couldn't hold back any longer. In my apartment one evening, I used the only tool I owned myself, my pitiful handheld, and started digging into police files. Sparse as they were, I found police log reports, but for the day of the fire, I found nothing. It was as though the event never occurred. No fire. No dispatcher calls. No activity reports. Nothing.

Same with the fire department, which wasn't a surprise since from time immemorial they had adopted "tight-lipped" as their office motto about anything, anytime. Apparently, the day of the fire, their equipment sat unused in all the fire stations, or at least that's what they wanted everyone to believe. No reports indicated action. Nothing.

Then, I connected Chase Cameron's mention of a fatality with the reality of death in the Borwyn fire. A fatality certainly should have generated a coroner's report and investigation. Again, nothing. Nada. I sat back, swallowed a generous sip of beer and continued to ponder what I had and didn't have. Maybe, it wasn't fatal. Didn't they find a body? Did they take it to a different jurisdiction?

But I realized if there was a body, they had to do something with it. So I dug into the transportation records of the coroner's meat wagon, and sure enough, on the day of the fire it had been used to transport the body of a deceased female from 112 Borwyn Street to the coroner's lab.

At lunchtime the following day, I walked to the county office tower again, but this time I didn't go up the stairs into the tower. Instead, I went around back to the coroner's building, a plain, one-story concrete box with no windows. I didn't waste my time with the front entrance and its prim receptionist behind thick glass, but I took a sideways path to a garage door on a narrow alley, with a single metal door. It was not locked.

Inside at a lone desk, I found an obese gentleman with receding hair, a beard, and an official-looking gray uniform. A white, gas-powered ambulance sat nearby. The place smelled of oil and gasoline.

"Do you drive that?" I asked.

"Yeah. You got a stiff that needs a ride?" the fat fellow said, chuckling at his own humor.

"No, but I would like to know about one that took a ride a few months ago. How's your memory?"

"It's okay. Who wants to know? And how much is it worth to ya?"

"I do. It was my, uh, cousin. She died in a fire. Here." I took out my cash money and tried a 50-dollar offering, which he quickly pulled from my fingers.

"'Kay. How far back?" He dug an ancient tablet out of a drawer and began pawing at it.

"Um, middle of last summer. The big building on Borwyn Street that burned down."

He made humming sounds and slowed his fingering. "Yeah. I remember that. Here 'tis. A woman. DOA. She was pretty crispy. We brought her here. Wanna see the pictures?"

I inhaled deeply to quell my nausea and decided I could go with this for now. I had a confirmed fatal fire. Now I had to decide what to do with the information. It wasn't really timely news, but at my workspace, I wrote up the facts anyway. To avoid blowback from the management, I waited until I had completed several other innocuous PR pieces, buried my little news item among them, and fed it all to the HAWG, which dutifully posted this:

> A fire at 112 Borwyn St. last summer claimed the life of a woman, coroner's records have revealed.
>
> An unidentified woman died in the fire, records indicate. Police and fire records are not available to determine a cause of death or the identity of the victim.
>
> The fire last July 31 destroyed the structure, causing an estimated five million dollars in damages. Its owner, Milo Proffitt, is now involved in litigation concerning sale of the property.

First thing the next morning, I got a message from Lucy Noble's desk, but it was someone else's voice. I was told I had to see Mr. Franco immediately, so I picked up my pad with notes about the road-paving projects and strolled down to his office. Lucy wasn't there, her place occupied by a skinny young black woman with beads in her braided hair.

"Where's Lucy?" I asked.

"She's no longer with the company," the woman said in an official tone.

"Yeah? That's a surprise," I said, and I wasn't kidding. "What happened?"

"She missed several days last week, so Mr. Franco let her go," the woman replied. "When she called, she said she was in the hospital."

"What? What happened? Which one?"

"Dunno." She swung her head slightly toward Franco's door. In rhythm, her beads rattled as her head turned. "He's waiting."

I opened the door and squinted with the bright sunlight shining through the big windows behind Mr. Franco at his desk. There being no chair, I stood waiting for him to look up. I feared that I knew what this was about. "You wanted to see me?" I said innocently.

"Did you post this yesterday about the fire on Borwyn?" he asked in his booming voice, elevated considerably above any normal conversation. He pointed at his monitor.

"Yes. I found some interesting—"

"Didn't I make it clear that you were to leave that stuff alone? Think you can ignore my directions? Let me say it one last time: you're not paid to be a journalist, and this fire stuff is really none of your business."

"Well, yes, I do think that's part of my job," I returned. "And it does seem to be interesting that it's been hidden from the public."

"You don't understand this stuff," Franco responded in an even more elevated tone. "If there are no records, it's for a reason. Now, I've told you several times to leave it alone. I meant that. Leave it." He released a heavy sigh, which seemed to calm him down a bit. "Look, we like you here. Those construction pieces were good work. Stick to that. You get into this other mess and bad things could start happening."

"Bad things? Like what?" I blurted.

Franco visibly tightened his jaw. "This is above you. You're just being annoying now. Don't be. We'll be keeping an eye on you, so get your work done and keep your nose out of places it doesn't belong."

As I left, I asked Franco's new gatekeeper for Lucy's contact information. She had nothing but an old phone card number. That night I called it. Lucy sounded surprised when I said hello, but without a screen, I couldn't tell how she really was.

After a few pleasantries, Lucy confessed that she wasn't doing so well. "I'm in a world of hurt," she said. "My boyfriend caught me outside of work and pounded me like it was another round in a prize fight. Put me in the hospital for days. Franco fired me when I couldn't come to work. Ended my contract. Can you believe it? Now I've got no income." She paused for a heartbeat before she added, "I'm being kicked out of my place. I'm gonna hafta find me and my little boy some place to stay. Know of anything?"

I knew I had to do it. My apartment wasn't big, but it had one bedroom, a living room, and furniture. And a roof, heat, and running water. "You can stay here at my place," I said without thinking, and within hours I had roommates.

It wasn't a bad situation. Daytimes, Lucy took her tubby five-year-old son, Jamaal, to school and then she looked for work. The pair slept in the living room on the couch and on an inflatable mat, and they cleaned up their mess each morning and put away their personal goods nicely. Food wasn't really a problem, because there were plenty of eating places nearby, and my weekly delivery provided more than enough for snacks and any light meals we wanted to whip up. Sometimes, Lucy even cooked a real dinner, as best she could, given the strange processed and boxed foodstuffs at hand.

Indy was fine with the situation, too. After all, Lucy had introduced Indy to me, and they were acquaintances, if not close friends. Indy would stop in every once in a while, play with the boy and chat with Lucy. Our little group settled in reasonably well. That is, until the situation got confused.

A couple weeks after Lucy and the boy arrived, I didn't get my week's food delivered. When I texted my complaint, they responded that my payment hadn't been transferred. No money, no food. I'd have to come in person and pay in cash.

Flustered, I had to arrange a rideshare to the food store halfway across town. When I got there, I confronted the counter clerk, a nice-looking young girl with emerald-green eyes and flaming-red hair. "Cash?" I asked. "Nobody pays in cash."

Her face opened up with a big, toothy smile. "Sorry. That's what your account says," she replied. "I'll be glad to put your order together and you can take it home, but I have to have cash payment first."

My stomach was growling louder than my voice, so I checked off my order form, paid, and stuffed my groceries in an old backpack. It was heavy, and I was tired when I got to my apartment, but I was surprised that the fake meat hadn't thawed much and the tofu packages hadn't split open. The only casualty was the bread, which had been crushed by a six-pack of beer bottles. But at least we could eat at home now.

The following week, I got a notice from the electric company that they hadn't received my most recent payment, either. I would be shut off if I didn't come up with the cash. *Immediately.* So I scrambled together some leftover funds and transmitted the payment, and when I checked my records, I found the original payment had been transferred as necessary, on time, but somehow it had been lost in processing. To recover my money, I had to spend an evening filling out forms for an appeal and send that to an office a couple hundred miles away.

As I sat back after filling out those forms, I wasn't satisfied. These annoying financial glitches couldn't be mere coincidence. I suspected someone was trying to make my life difficult. I was determined to find out what was happening to me.

VII

A few weeks later, Indy and I met for an evening at a nice café she had selected. The walls, painted flat black, and the dark window drapes pulled closed contrasted with the white tablecloths and wavering candlelight at each table. Indy's dark mood matched the decor. She complained that her father had been pestering her with messages. He wanted Indy to begin testing for what he called a medical "procedure" that would solve a hereditary health issue.

"Doesn't he talk to you in person?" I asked. "Doesn't he explain what this is all about?"

"He's been hinting about this for years," Indy replied. "Lately he's been sending me a lot of little 'reminders.'" She emphasized with air quotes. "Or I hear him creaking up the stairs. He'll stand outside my room with the door closed and ask if I've done anything yet. Doesn't even bother to open the door."

"You sure it isn't a ghost?" I mused, trying to lighten up the conversation. The effort dropped like a wet bag of sand.

"I wish it were. All I know is Father gave me a specialist's name and ID number. I'm supposed to set up an appointment and get the lowdown. But I feel just fine. Don't I look okay?"

Before I could answer, Chase the lawyer approached our table. "Indy! Great to see you!" he said enthusiastically, and I invited him to join us.

"What's new with you?" he aimed at Indy.

"My father's being a jerk," she said. "I'm thinking of moving out, to a place of my own."

I gasped a little at this news, then stashed it in the back of my mind and changed the subject. "How's the legal business, Chase?" I said.

"Hey, I remember you from my skating party last winter."

"I still have the bruised butt to remind me."

"Don't you work for InfoNet Now?" Chase asked. "That's what's happening with legal business. The conglomerate that owns you finally settled up with the owner of the rubble on Borwyn. He got pennies. I hear the conglomerate's going to build a frou-frou glamorous student recreation center and lease it to the university."

"Didn't somebody die in the fire?" I asked. "That didn't hold up the proceedings?"

"Apparently not. They closed on the deal yesterday."

Mystified, the journalist in me pushed a little harder. "Hmm. No fire inspector's investigation?"

"Criminal law is on the other side of the hall," Chase responded. "So, Indy, how's your tennis game?"

We joked a bit about that, because Indy's game had taken an expensive turn. She was used to thrashing me regularly, but my tennis had improved to the extent that I could at least compete with her, which she didn't like. She often stomped her feet and screamed at the demon ball if I made a decent play. One time, after I had swatted a good shot past her into a corner of the court, she halted, squinted her eyes, cursed, and beat her racket on the court until it shattered. The tantrum stunned me, not just because she disintegrated a high-end stick, but also because Indy momentarily became a different person. "I guess I really lost it." She chuckled with Chase and me. "That racket cost a fortune."

The next morning, feeding the HAWG kept me busy at work. Some residents of an outlying community had complained to InfoNet Now about a new hydroponic vegetable-growing facility near their neighborhood. They claimed the company was releasing water polluted by extremely high nutrients and other materials into a small stream. That befouled fluid was flowing into a nearby formerly pristine trout stream, ruining the water quality and the fishing opportunities. The community relied on well fields around the stream for its water supply, and they gained some income from wealthy anglers who had been visiting the area for sport. We contacted the vegetable company and got lots of information: quotes and high-quality 3-D video on the efficiency of the operation, the number of jobs it supported, the foods it produced in abundance for local restaurants, and of course their attention to the environment, all of which we fed into the HAWG. The company didn't mention that it had arranged for protesters from the community to be hauled into criminal court for trespassing.

The light bulb in my head clicked on when I uncovered those criminal court files while digging up information for the hydroponic story. Chase Cameron had said the night before that the criminal law team across the hall was handling the Borwyn Street building fire. That meant the death must have been a crime, not an accident, and that meant the incident became local crime news. Mug shots and perp walks drew lots of eyeballs, so InfoNet Now loved local crime stories. If I could get details, maybe the fire story would get some traction in our organization.

So at my noon break, after the HAWG regurgitated copy that we posted, I trotted down to see Miss Hinders at the government records center. It was raining hard, and I was soaking wet when I found her in the same basement cubbyhole, scanning documents, and she was just as welcoming as she had been on our first encounter.

"You here again? Been swimming?" she asked with a ho-hum voice. "What this time?"

"I'm looking for police reports about the fire on Borwyn Street last summer," I replied. "They should be pretty easy to find."

But they weren't. The Borwyn fire didn't exist, according to the police activity logs.

"Hmm, that's odd," Miss Hinders said as she led me to the Municipal Fire Inspector records, after I greased her palm with another 10-dollar bill, of course. I found nothing there, either. Yet something did happen on Borwyn Street. I was there. I saw it. This was bewildering.

VIII

The memo popped up on my screen at midmorning a day later. The first couple lines stunned me, and I really don't remember much beyond them:

> A recent review of your work product indicates its quality meets our requirements, and we are pleased to continue our relationship with you. However, it has been determined that the extent of your contract exceeds our current needs. Therefore, pursuant to the employment agreement in effect, your required service hours will be reduced by 50 percent weekly.

The words hit me like a forehand smash off a bad lob. I was stunned.

"Bowman," I blurted, "did you get one of these memos that cut your hours by half?"

He answered without even looking up. "What? No, of course not. What are you talking about?"

"Here it is. I'm being cut in half. What's going on?" I was babbling now.

"Geez, that's tough," Bowman said. "You must have really pissed somebody off. What'd you do?"

In my mind, I was calculating lost income, and I pulled up my contract to review its language. Sure enough, it said InfoNet Now would decide how much I worked or didn't work, and that could be changed at will. Their will. I was screwed.

My only thought was "Why?" I was a good content provider; I did good work. I wasn't pushy, except maybe when I followed my intuition about that fire . . . and then a feeling of dread washed over me. How much about my curiosity did my bosses know? Why would they care so much?

That night I went home to my apartment and took a mental inventory of my possessions. I lived a comfortable life, certainly not opulent like Indy, but well enough. But in a week rent would be due, and after that my income wouldn't match my lifestyle. The one-bedroom apartment would have to go, and with it, probably my cushy furniture. Surely, I could keep the bed, my tennis gear and some clothes, and maybe some dishes and utensils. Nothing else.

Of course, the situation also affected Lucy and Jamaal. That evening, I told Lucy they'd have to move on, news that she took surprisingly well. She said she had some leads on employment, so she was feeling optimistic. Besides, she wasn't surprised.

"I hafta tell you, I thought you'd get canned," Lucy said. "Get with it. They can make your life miserable if you're doing something they don't like. I know that from experience. You . . . you don't know when to stop poking around. You stirred up the hornet's nest and now you've been stung.

"I've moved beyond InfoNet Now," she added. "On the horizon, I can see a place of my own. I've got other friends. You need to broaden your horizon, too. Stop being so obsessed. I'd hate to see more bad things happen to you." Lucy gave me a small smile. "We'll get out of your hair as soon as we can."

Which they did. In a matter of a few days, Lucy had found housing in a temporary shelter for women. When we said our goodbyes, she told me she had an interview later in the day for a good job.

"You saved my ass," she said. "I owe you. You've been good to us. It was even fun once in a while." With that, we shared a hug, and she and Jamaal turned and walked out, carrying their possessions in their arms and backpacks. I felt a little sorry to see them go.

A week or so later, I found a room I could afford. It was quite a few train stops out in the suburbs, and it didn't have the dramatic view of the city I enjoyed from my apartment. The new place at one time had been temporary living quarters for business people, with a sparse bathroom, space for a small desk and chair, room for a bed, and even a little kitchen-like space, and that was it. It smelled faintly of natural gas coming from the old furnace and the amateur paint job that had been applied to refresh the place, and it was noisy because a major roadway passed right outside its two front windows. But if I had a vehicle, which I didn't, I could have parked it right in front of my new flat.

I arranged to give away all my property that wouldn't fit in the new place, and it distressed me to watch the workers cart out the stuff of my life. My comfy lounge chair, my sofa, my antique dresser, all gone to new homes. I don't think I had ever felt so helpless. When the crew finished carting my bed and desk into my new apartment, I stood in the doorway and looked around. This was going to be a depressing new lifestyle, I thought. But the place fit my truncated budget, and this would be where I would have to live for the foreseeable future.

That night, I flopped onto my bed in my claustrophobic hovel, tired and depressed. But the more I thought about how I had been put in this situation, the angrier I got. Someone didn't want me stirring the ashes of that fire on Borwyn Street, and now I wanted to know who and why. So, I used my handheld to look up the county taxing office and found the name of the former owner of the Borwyn Street building, Milo Proffitt. For years, he had fought a holding action in court against the state university and the state government, the entities that coveted his property. If I had been taking this line of query seriously, he should have been one of the first sources to contact. Now, I was serious. I used a voice connection on my handheld and called him.

"Yeah, it was mine," his voice said. He had shut off the video at his end, so I couldn't see him. "Why are you asking? What do you want?"

I explained that I was a content provider for InfoNet Now and that I was working up a story.

"That's a joke," he responded. "Especially for InfoNet Now. Your company is in this up to their necks. Anything about that property will be buried so deep a groundhog couldn't find it.

"I was making money off the building," he continued. "It was a popular place. Had nice apartments and nice little shops. But the state wanted that property. And they got it.

"Listen, the walls have eyes and ears. If you want to talk, don't call me; I'll contact you. Okay?"

Then, he shut off.

Because my work hours had been cut, midmorning the next day, I was sitting at my little desk in my little apartment when an old-fashioned email popped up on my handheld. Proffitt wrote that he would meet me in person, if I came alone and agreed not to take notes or capture any images.

He insisted we meet at a site far out in the suburbs. I took a train, then hoofed it to the rendezvous point, one of those vast spaces left behind by lost "shopping destinations," empty but for sparse weeds fighting up through cracks in the pavement. I found him sitting in an old gas truck parked amid huge piles of concrete, bricks, and mortar, all that remained of what once had been an anchor department store.

I knocked on a window, and a little fellow inside whipped around with eyes wide open, as if I'd surprised him. "You Mr. Avila?" he asked through the closed window. When I assured him I was, and confirmed my identity by holding my content-provider license up to the window, he popped open the door and invited me in.

Proffitt wasn't at all what I expected. A short, bald fellow, he wore a checkered flannel shirt dominated by red- and cream-colored squares, loose blue denim jeans, and a rumpled black sport coat.

"So you wanna talk about my building?" he said in a voice more squeaky than I detected over the phone.

"Yeah," I answered as I climbed in. "What's with all this secrecy?"

"Listen," Proffitt said. "You can't be too careful. You don't know what you're dealing with here."

"Yeah, I've had a hard time finding things," I said. "I really had to dig to find out about the fire in your building. Why is everything so hidden?"

"Who are you kidding? Haven't you figured it out? They wanted my building. They couldn't get it in city council, or in court, so they made sure the property would be worthless. They won.

"We had a nice little community there. A bakery. A coffee shop. Some offices. A couple nice apartments. They wiped it out."

I said it was a shame the neighborhood had lost its core, but he had made some money on the deal, so it didn't seem like he'd been hurt too badly. "But here's my real question," I continued. "Did you know somebody died in the fire?"

"Of course. Knew her well. She worked for the security company I hired. Her name was Chanya Gheni. Nice girl. It's a tragedy. But the people who took the property now don't care that they killed her. They didn't care who they hurt, as long as they got their damn property."

"So you think the fire was deliberately set, do you? You sure she didn't just get caught in the wrong place at the wrong time?"

Proffitt's voice took on a disturbed tone. "I wasn't making a metaphor," he answered. "I mean Chanya died because they killed her. That fire was set."

I bit my tongue. "You have any proof?"

"Look. I heard from my insurance company—and I had to twist arms to get even this—that the fire started in three places at about the same time. In an office and storage area I was renting out, in a trash bin that somebody moved, and in the bakery kitchen. But they've kept that information out of sight. Try and find anything in the official reports about it." He scanned the area through the window. "And first, before the fire, they threatened me. After court one time, one of their stooges told me I better settle or there wouldn't be anything left to settle."

I was having a hard time holding all this together. The thought occurred to me that Mr. Proffitt was off his rocker. Paranoid, certainly.

"Wait a minute. Who's this 'they' you keep talking about? Who is 'they'?"

Proffitt jumped at the question as though he had been released from a cage. He said he believed a small group of powerful people, political and business leaders, "controlled everything: government, business, universities, the whole fabric of society." He described a series of interlocking boards, legal entities and controlling directorates, and the individuals who led them, including Paul Lexar, Indy's father and the head of InfoNet Now.

"So, they just bought their way in?" I suggested, trying to fill in the blank spaces.

"How naive," Proffitt said. "It isn't money. I have money. How could I afford the gas for this truck if I didn't? No, it's making sure family connections continue. Legacy. It's like these people, because they're sons or daughters, they get into this secret club. It just goes on. You rarely see them. You just feel the results of their decisions. Like the lost records you tried to find.

"They manipulate the rules. They get what they want. They know how to get it, regardless of the human cost," he said. "Doesn't matter who or what's in their way. It's like they have no conscience, just ways to get control.

"And they're always one step ahead of the rest of us."

Proffitt stopped abruptly, like he had come to a precipice that he dared not go over. He reached for the truck's controls, pressed a button, and loudly announced, "Start." The gas engine rumbled to life.

"I've said way too much already," he said hurriedly. "Gotta go." He pressed another button and the door behind me popped open so quickly that I almost fell out backward.

I got the hint, expressed my thanks, and continued to roll out.

"You be careful," Proffitt said as he closed the door. The truck sped off, scattering gravel and leaving me to retrace my many steps back across the hot, barren asphalt to the train and eventually to my room.

Two days later, InfoNet Now called me in for some rewrite work. Bowman and I were busy reorganizing a news release about a local health benefits provider. I was shoveling it into the HAWG when Bowman took a break to check some news feeds.

"Huh. Here's a rarity these days," Bowman said. "Fatal car crash. No, wait. Not a collision. It says the guy apparently had a medical attack of some kind while speeding. His gas truck went off the highway and into a tree."

"Too bad," I said. "That's what he gets for driving a gas truck. E-pods just don't crash these days."

"Any identity of the victim?" I asked, without thinking much.

"Yeah. A pretty well-known businessman. Name's Milo Proffitt."

IX

I didn't think Proffitt's crash was a coincidence. When I finished my rewrite work, I left the building, stopped at a coffee shop, and used my handheld to check police records on the accident. It didn't surprise me that there weren't any. So I dodged puddles from a rain shower en route to the police station, got buzzed in through the security door after I relayed a fiction of myself as a public relations person looking to do a story about the captain on duty, and approached the duty sergeant. A clearly bored, corpulent older fellow sitting behind thick security glass, he barely raised his eyes when he asked my purpose for standing there. After I described the gas truck accident and the victim, he pawed at a virtual keyboard, rolled in his chair over to another screen, rolled back to the thick glass, and pronounced that incident out of bounds because of continuing investigation. I knew I wasn't going to breach that wall. I said thank you, turned on my heel, and departed for the coroner's office, where I got the same result. Someone didn't want details of that accident to be known.

That evening, I walked in the misty, gathering darkness to a restaurant where Indy had asked me to meet her after work. I took wary steps, carefully studying every dark alley and doorway, and twisting my head frequently to see if I was being followed. I had thought Proffitt was something of a paranoid nut, but now I was beginning to surrender to fears of my own.

Indy and I had not seen each other for a couple of weeks, since just before I moved, so I was looking forward to a nice evening. The place where we were to meet specialized in seafood, something I was never able to afford, but Indy liked the place, with its fake maritime atmosphere and nautical aroma of cooked fish. She always seemed to look forward to inviting me there. That's why I was a little concerned when she arrived a quarter hour late, with her eyes moist and face red and puffy.

I struggled to say something appropriate when she sat down. Words wouldn't come to mind, though, a real problem for someone who claims to be a writer.

"What's up?" was all I could say.

"Nothing I can't deal with on my own."

Honesty, I thought, might be the best approach. "It doesn't look like nothing," I said in a matter-of-fact way. It was the wrong strategy.

"Listen. If you're going to interrogate me, I don't need that," Indy responded through her gritted, perfectly straight and perfectly white teeth. "I'll just leave."

"No, no, no," I whispered. "I'm just trying to show some empathy."

"You can't empathize with my problem," she responded. "It's pretty unique."

A short woman with ink-black hair and too much makeup appeared, tablet in hand, and asked for drink preferences. Indy ordered red wine, and I asked for their house beer. When the drinks arrived, Indy gulped her wine in a couple of long draughts. She ordered another.

Before long I heard the explanation. "I've been having a lot of trouble with my father," she said. "Really, not my father. His messages. He's been pestering me night and day to get this 'family problem' thing done. Makes no sense to me. I feel fine. I look okay, don't I?"

"Uh, great."

"He wanted me to go to this special clinic place. I said no. He insisted. Again and again. One time, he even used voice messaging, and I could tell he was really angry. Yelling at me that I was stubborn. I just didn't understand.

"Then about a week ago, I got a message from him that he was tired of me dragging my feet. Fact is, I wasn't just dragging my feet, I was trying to ignore him. But the message said two of his technicians would stop by to visit me. They would discuss my options.

"Sure enough, that evening two people showed up. Big, muscular girls dressed in white medical-looking outfits. One with dark, curly hair just pushed her way into my place and the other followed. 'We're here for you,' she said, and I said I didn't know what they were talking about. 'Don't you know this is for your own good?' the curly one said. The other one, a blonde who was a little shorter than the curly one, grabbed my left arm, and none too gently, I might add. I told her to get her hands off me. She called me 'honey' and said something about 'cooperating with the company.'"

Indy said the bigger woman took a step toward her, so Indy stepped back, which was right into the arms of the blonde. Indy remembered that the curly-haired one said something like "Sorry about this, but we have to," and lifted a can to her face and sprayed a cool, medicinal-smelling mist at her. Indy said she started twisting to get away, but almost immediately, felt heavy and out of sorts, like her brain had been loosened and twisted. She said she tried to stay standing, but her legs softened "like cooked spaghetti," and she dropped. She didn't recall hitting the floor, though. She guessed her visitors caught her.

"I remember a very rough ride in some kind of vehicle," Indy continued. "I tried to wiggle, but the two women told me to stay still, and I didn't have any strength anyway. Next thing I knew, I was in a brightly lit room with tubes in my arms and people washing me. They were talking about blood pressure and breathing, stuff like that. Then, I really drifted off to a deep sleep.

"I woke up a time or two. Once a doctor, or some kind of professional in medical clothes, sat next to me and explained that they had performed a procedure and that it had gone well. My father had signed off on it. I'd be in pain, the guy said, so they had given me drugs. Then I drifted off.

"When I woke up, I was in my own bed, in my apartment," Indy said. "The big woman was beside me, dressed in her medical smock. She said I'd had a reaction to a medicine my father had ordered for me, and they had to take me to a clinic ahead of schedule for this emergency procedure."

Indy's voice broke when she described all this, and I could understand why. She said she told the woman to get out of her place, that she could take care of herself, and the woman did so. "Strange, she didn't say a word," Indy reported. Indy said she then climbed out of bed, even though she felt like she had her worst hangover ever, found her handheld, and put in a call to her father's office.

"When I told the guy who answered who I was, and that I wanted to speak to my father, he immediately said they had heard about my mishap and wished me well," she said. "Now, that was weird. How did they know? Then, he said my father wasn't available, but he'd get back to me soon.

"That was a few days ago. I haven't heard from him yet. I contacted the police after I called my father, because I wasn't going to stand for this. They took my name, address, and my story, and they said an investigator would get back to me. Nothing yet. Then I called you to meet me here tonight."

I felt like I should take notes, because her story seemed so compelling. The dark-haired waitress delivered steaming plates of authentic-looking seafood, and Indy and I continued to exchange ideas about what could have happened, and why. Indy said she couldn't understand all the health concerns, because she felt worse than before the incident. She dropped her fork several times as we dined, and she admitted she found simple motor skills more difficult now.

And strange things were being sent to her. Indy said a large unsolicited file had been downloaded to her from InfoNet Now, and she discovered that it included a message from her father explaining that he had the contents assembled from old family treasures. She started to review them and discovered dozens of old home videos and images.

"There's lots more," she said. "Come over to my place tonight, and we'll have drinks and revisit my family. Here, touch my handheld. I'll transfer your fingerprints to my security system so you can get in."

I didn't need to be asked twice. I recorded my prints on her handheld, and later that evening, I used that identity to seamlessly gain entry to her new downtown-apartment building, where I caught a glass-enclosed elevator to the 30th floor. Hers was the only living space on the floor. When I touched her security pad, the door slid open, revealing Indy standing in front of a wall of huge floor-to-ceiling windows that presented itself from the foyer. The view surrounded us with a panorama of tiny lights spreading in all directions to the horizon. I was dazzled.

"Nice, isn't it?" Indy asked. "It's got a couple bedrooms and a working kitchen, plus a space down that hall for a live-in housekeeper if I hire one. I'm thinking of bringing in Ana Maria if I can get her away from my father's place. She'd have her own door and everything. It would be like her own place.

"Get us some cold drinks from the kitchen and make yourself comfortable while I kick off these dreadful shoes. I've got some neat stuff to show you."

I located wineglasses, poured Riesling from a bottle I found in the refrigerator, then plopped myself down on Indy's cushy sofa. I was surrounded by furniture of almost unimaginable grace: a wooden end table that appeared to be made of real mahogany, polished to a dark shine; a leather-bound, overstuffed lounge chair with subtle switches for adjustments on its side; and soft lights that dangled from the ceiling on cords I guessed to be 10 feet long.

Indy returned and dropped onto the couch, holding a small black device with lots of buttons. "Check this out," she said, and a frame unrolled from the ceiling. "My father sent this to me a couple weeks ago. It's our family history."

At that, images appeared before me in a fascinating revue. Professional-quality software had manipulated old family videos into three-dimensional projections that cavorted before us like assorted stage plays. We saw Indy as a child, running across the apartment floor to a young, dark-haired woman. "That's my mother. She was gone before I knew her," Indy said matter-of-factly. A gray-haired, somewhat uncomfortable-looking man, whom I took to be her father toyed with family dogs, flipping a ball that bounded off the screen toward us, then transformed magically into a tennis ball that teenage Indy and friends played.

That faded into a cavalcade of sports shots featuring her father, first as a very young man in old-style football uniforms, through college days, and then into clips of his professional playing days. I guessed those videos of the pro games were somewhat newer, maybe 50 years old or so, and the image quality was much finer. Most were close-ups of the man as a young athlete in his prime, carrying the ball over giant defenders who seemed to battle right in front of us, or scampering from side to side in Indy's living room. "No wonder lawsuits smothered the sport," I whispered. "Look at them blast one another."

I thought of myself as a pretty good content provider, but the quality of this visual narrative astounded me. The shots seamlessly blended from one memory to another, with no hint of digital manipulation. Yet, I found the grainy older images less appealing, with one brief scene especially puzzling. A long shot zoomed out from Indy's father dashing across an old high school football gridiron, and for a split second, what seemed to be a car parking lot appeared in the distance, except gas vehicles from the mid-twentieth century filled the lot. That was more than a century ago. Maybe it was antique car show, I thought.

Throughout the video, Indy narrated. "That was my first dog," she'd say, or "my mom seemed to like those flowered prints." Meanwhile, I allowed my fingers to explore the crook of her elbow at my side, the soft hairs on her firm bicep, then the silky softness of the nape of her neck. She didn't seem to mind and snuggled closer as the images danced in front of us.

Then my fingers encountered an aberration, a barely perceptible rise on an otherwise smooth landscape. I peeked at her neck and discovered a little sensor near her hairline at the nape of her neck.

"What's this thing?" I asked.

"I got that during my little adventure at the clinic. I don't know what it is—can't see the back of my neck. I remember they did turn me over to attach some tubes. They said they had to record my vitals. It's some kind of port."

"You'll have it permanently?" I asked.

The show in front of us was ending, with shots of a grown-up Indy and Ana Maria at their house with the tennis court backyard, so I turned my attention to further explore Indy's physique. I playfully found the zipper on the back of her blouse, conveniently starting at the mysterious port, and pulled it.

"Hey, be careful of the sutures," was all Indy said.

"Seems like you're being monitored," I said. "Who's doing this? Why?"

"It's this family thing."

"You believe too much. Don't be so naive."

"What do you mean, 'naive'? I don't think I like that. I'm not stupid."

"Whoa, I don't mean anything by it. It's just that, well, it looks to me like you're being set up physically for something. Like you're a lab rat."

"I'm not a lab rat."

"A lab rat can't say no. Seems like you can't, either."

"You implying that I *want* this to happen? Listen, John, didn't you hear me that two big women carried me out? And I called the police on my own father, didn't I?"

"Yeah, for nothing. I wouldn't trust your father. He's having something done to you. I don't think it's right, and I'd bet it's not legal. How far are you willing to go to make him stop? You gonna take him to court? Have him arrested for kidnapping?"

"What do you mean, 'don't trust'? He's my father. What makes you think he'd want to hurt me?"

"Dunno. Maybe he wants to control you. Maybe he wants to run you like a robot." I chuckled at my own humor. "Maybe he wants to make you part of the team."

Indy didn't laugh. "You've gone over the edge now. Nobody's gonna run my life like that."

"Well, it seems like your father's trying to. He wants you in his group. You know, the people in control. You're most of the way there now anyway."

"What do you mean by that remark?" Indy asked with a snarl.

"Oh, come on. Look around you, Indy. Not many people live like this."

"I paid for all this with my own money!" Indy was getting angry now. "I earned it!"

I don't think she realized the irony in her remark. "Face it," I said. "You're wealthy. You've been mouthing the silver spoon since you were born."

"I don't have to listen to this," Indy said, her voice rising several decibels. I had seen this version of Indy before, and it wasn't pretty. "What do you know? You're just a content provider."

"I know what I see, and I can see that you're being manipulated. Probably illegally."

"You're accusing my father of being a crook? That's absurd. He may be eccentric, but he's not evil."

"Um, he always gets his way. And it looks to me like he's doing something to his own daughter that isn't right."

"I think maybe you better go now," she said abruptly.

"Aw, c'mon. You can't run away from the truth."

"That's it. Out. Now!"

I knew when to retreat, and now was that time. I stepped away and muttered, "Sorry. Bye," as I slipped out the door, leaving Indy sitting on the sofa. I could just about see the steam hissing from her ears.

I sat befuddled during the long train ride to the suburbs and then in my little room. I admit I stared at the walls and ceiling a lot that night. As the clock showed single digits, I wrestled with myself, thinking about what I had said, or shouldn't have said. Eventually, I dozed but only briefly, until the morning light streamed through the two windows that broke up the wall on either side of my door.

I was preparing a morning coffee when my handheld beeped with a message. It was Indy, saying she felt "terrible" about how she had acted last night. "I was such a jerk," she said. "I'm coming out there to apologize." This surprised me, because up to then, she had not taken the initiative to visit my place. Nevertheless, the message delighted me, and I admit it made me feel a bit smug. And it set me to hustling about arranging the clutter. I made my bed, organized my books, and then tidied the scrabble of notes that filled my little desk. I left the tiny kitchenette a mess. There wasn't much more to attend to.

A half hour later, as I sat at my desk chair reviewing some notes, I heard the *whirr* of an e-pod outside my windows. I jumped up, and a second later, heard the knock at my door. I put on a bright smile.

But when I opened the door, I saw Indy's face fall into a frown. She peered in, her eyes looking down and ahead, as though she feared stepping into a mud puddle. "Uh, long way out here," she said. Then she moved forward, out of the bright sunlight of the morning, and with one scan, she took in the brevity of my room.

She halted abruptly, arms at her side slightly spread with palms forward, as though she had hit an unseen barrier. She didn't say a word. Then she stepped straight backward in mini-steps until she had cleared the doorway.

"What's the matter?" was all I could mutter. "Something wrong?"

"You live in *this?*" Indy said, with an incredulous emphasis on the last word. "I . . . I . . . I, uh, just have to go. Sorry."

She slid under the car door, which had remained open, and it dropped shut. The lights illuminated, the e-pod backed away, and wheels spit up gravel as Indy drove off.

I didn't know what to do. Confused, I staggered back into my room and lay on the bed, where I reviewed what had just happened. Sometime later—maybe a half hour, I don't know—I sent Indy a text, and then left a message on an audio line. Neither got a response. I'd visit her the next day, I thought. Yes, the next day. Not now. I had no work to occupy my mind, so for the rest of the day, I wandered around. I checked messages frequently, read a book absent-mindedly, and rolled up a burrito with beans and really bad fake cheese, but I wasn't hungry anyway. Then, a message came and I scrambled to open it. It was only Bowman asking me to come in to work the next day. He sent me some texts to work on.

That interlude at least got my mind off Indy and into a little writing project, which the HAWG could have done just about as easily. But it distracted me for the following morning when I dropped in at the office, and it provided a little income. On the train home I thought of how to dress, and what to say, for my all-important visit to Indy later in the day.

I had the words assembled when I arrived at my place and found a small light-green envelope taped to my door. Aside from the sheer tradition of the handwritten note enclosed, the contents would have been funny, in a literary sense, had they not stuck in my throat: "Dear John," it said, followed by a few pleasantries. Then Indy gently pierced my heart: "You must understand," she wrote, "that the future is not for us to be together." There were a few more words, and her signature, but that was it.

✕

Indy's departure extinguished the spark of my life. For weeks, I moped about, unable to focus on much of anything. I lost weight. I admit that when Bowman called me in to help edit copy, I used my visit into the city as an excuse to wander the streets at night, peering into restaurants I couldn't afford, hoping to catch a glimpse of Indy. One time, I was sure I spied her, sitting with friends at a candlelit table near the front window of a place we had visited often. I pulled away instantly, lest I be caught in my stalking.

It took about three weeks, but eventually meaning returned to my days. Work filled my time enough to keep my mind off Indy, and one morning as I organized some mindless puff pieces, a command from above appeared on my screen. Mr. Franco ordered that we drop everything and prepare a big promo package on a new project that was rising up from the ashes of the burned-out edifice at 112 Borwyn Street. Soon, the fact sheet said, university students would enjoy the luxuries of first-class dining, recreational facilities, and top-tier luxury suites, all prepared by a general contractor that was an InfoNet Now subsidiary.

"Those pampered kids don't need more of that," I complained. Bowman nodded in agreement.

"They're born into such wealth," he said. "They have the best clothes, the finest e-pods out in the parking lots, and now this. Do they ever work? Are they ever really challenged?"

Of course, my thoughts turned quickly to Indy, Chase Cameron, and the crowd among whom I had once mingled. And Paul Lexar, Indy's father, and a force on the university board of trustees through InfoNet Now. Then, I made the connection to Milo Proffitt and his observation that what the university trustees wanted, they got. They had wanted that Borwyn Street property, and they got it. Surely the members of that board knew that the place had been destroyed by fire. And what about the fatality? Didn't anyone care?

My renewed curiosity compelled me to learn the truth. I looked up my notes from the Proffitt interview and found the name of the fire victim, Chanya Gheni. Then, I started digging in directories. The name popped up in a few places, but without addresses; like most common people, the family apparently didn't own a home. But Chanya, according to Proffitt, had been a security guard. Maybe she had connections with the police, maybe even the day the building caught fire.

One cop who had been at the fire for sure was the woman who chased me away. Banks of low-hanging clouds the color of burned charcoal threatened rain as I traipsed over to the downtown police station, where I found the same bored, corpulent old sergeant behind thick security glass. There weren't many women on the force, I thought, so it would be easy to find the annoying officer.

"Why do you want her?" the bulbous fellow asked. He seemed satisfied when I explained that I needed information about a case she had worked on, and within minutes, she swung open the institutional-green metal door into the little entry room.

"Wadda ya want?" she asked. I remembered her as being taller than the person who stood before me now.

"You remember the fire in the big building on Borwyn Street about a year ago? I'm a content provider. I was there. You were there. You chased me away."

"So?"

"So, I heard somebody died in that fire. A security guard. She didn't happen to send an alarm or anything, did she?"

"Yep, she did. I got dispatched on that call. Damn shame about her. Then, I had to tell her family 'cause I was the woman on the scene." She shook her head, her loose, dark hair swishing side to side. "Why do they do that? Why am I always the one?"

I lurched at this information. "You talked to the family? How did you find them?"

"The building owner told us. They lived way out in the burbs, off Route 35 West. Hey, yer not going to mess with 'em, are you?"

"No, no, nothing like that. I, uh, I'm doing a story on the new building that's going up where the fire happened," I answered. It was the truth, sort of. "Thanks. You gave me the information I needed."

Indeed she had. Among all the Gheni names only one lived at an address on Route 35 West, way beyond the city limits. I took the train out as far as I could, then paid for a rideshare to a tiny house, one of hundreds of identical little brick one-story houses built about a century ago for impoverished factory workers. But I was disappointed when the woman who answered the door, a well-dressed, middle-aged matronly type, said the Gheni family no longer lived there.

"They didn't take very good care of the place," the woman said. "I rented it to them for years; then suddenly, about six weeks ago, they ran into some money. Took off faster than rabbits. Left the place a mess. You lookin' to rent it?"

"No, no. I'm looking for the family. Didn't tell you where they went, did they?"

"Yeah, they had the nerve to ask for their security deposit back. And they sure stepped up in society," the matron said. "They moved in close to the city, into one of those new condos along the river. Here's the number."

She typed in some numbers on her handheld and transmitted them to mine. I thanked her profusely, called another rideshare, then took the train, and eventually found myself standing in front of a townhouse-style condominium building, spotlessly new, but featureless and rather plain in neutral colors. Its large front windows faced the river, now brown at near flood stage and ugly with floating trash, while around back I could see the construction equipment of a company that I knew from many articles I had written. Mud and thin brown grass struggling to gain a foothold comprised the landscaping.

A small, dark-complexioned woman answered my knock quickly. When I identified myself, she said that yes, the late Chanya Gheni had been a member of this family. Without apparent antagonism or remorse, the woman invited me into a bright, barren front room littered with large cardboard boxes that served as furniture. Dishes, half-empty cups, and a framed image of a young girl in a uniform sat on the floor among them. A slim young man, dark and handsome in his late teens, entered the room from stairs leading off to the side and asked if he could help. They both confirmed that Chanya had enjoyed her security job in Proffitt's building, but they could say no more because of a legal agreement they had signed. A well-dressed man and woman had visited them about six months after Chanya's death, they said, with a document offering a huge amount of money—they wouldn't say how much—if every member of the family would sign. But the rub was silence: the woman, the young man, and six other members of the family who signed had to clam up about anything having to do with Chanya's employment, the fire, and pretty much everything they knew about the whole tragedy. They took the money, kept Chanya in their memories, bought the condo where we now conversed, and moved happily into it.

The Ghenis offered to show me their new digs. They proudly led me first into an entertainment room, then to a little kitchen-like area, and then a utility room. Upstairs featured three bedrooms, they said, while downstairs, an unfinished basement awaited their designs. The head contractor (whom I had quoted in an InfoNet Now piece some years ago) had nicely offered to build into the condo amenities undreamed of by the Ghenis until now.

I knew enough to leave at that point. Bribery had twisted the Gheni family members into walking, talking public relations reps for the InfoNet Now conglomerate. Clearly, they weren't going to provide any more real information; indeed, their silence had been purchased thoroughly. But their calendar and their move yielded all the clues I had sought: the legal team offered the buyout even before InfoNet Now wrenched the burned-out property from Proffitt, who apparently recognized the takeover scheme before he died. Then, the conglomerate got some of its money back when it sold one of its properties to the Ghenis at a steep discount. The whole affair had been as neatly packaged as a birthday gift, bought with the life of at least one person, probably two. I began to see the dimensions of the corrupt package coming into focus. Now, I just needed to know who fashioned it. But I felt like I was inching closer to what really happened in 112 Borwyn Street.

XI

That evening, I returned to my little room, satisfied that I had unearthed important information. I set up my handheld so it cast its image on the wall behind my little desk and allowed myself the freedom to tap out some notes. They showed a path formed from covetous university trustees, through losing court cases, and to a fire that reduced the property they desired to charred rubble. Proffitt, before he died, told me the conflagration had been set. That made Chanya Gheni a murder victim. Proffitt, too, probably. My bravado influenced me to try to sleep with one eye open that night, but before long I dozed soundly.

My handheld interrupted that sleep with a buzz the following morning. This was no ordinary message: I was being called into the office of Paul Lexar. Surely, the head of the corporation didn't care what an underling like me had to say, I thought. This summons baffled me.

I had never seen him, or even heard his voice for that matter, so when an assistant ushered me through the door to his office, I didn't know what to expect. I entered a dark, surreal environment. Although he occupied a deluxe corner suite, window shades had been pulled down to block almost

all outside light, while inside, dim lamps cast a pitiful illumination, if it could be called even that.

Only when my pupils had adjusted to the faint wisps of
light was I able to see that someone else occupied the room.
Paul Lexar sat in front of a fireplace to the side of the room,
poking at coals and a small flame. The ashes glowed a bit,
providing enough luminance to cast a faint orange light on
his face. I could see his profile: a square chin, thick lips, a
patrician nose, and dusky, bushy black eyebrows over dark
eyes enhanced by the shadows. He wore a simple golf shirt.

"Fire is such an interesting thing, isn't it?" he spoke
slowly, with a deep, raspy voice. "Is flame a real thing or
just a vapor?"

I thought it odd to tend a fire in a fireplace, when
outside it was pretty warm. He didn't turn to look at me as
he continued, slowly.

"You know, the ability to manipulate fire is what sets
humans apart from the lower creatures." I was pretty sure
he was setting me up. I kept my mouth shut.

"I called you in here to tell you, personally, that your
insubordination has cost you your job. I want you out of
here today."

I figured the fireplace was a pretty blatant hint that he
knew what I was investigating, and I instantly recognized the
futility of my position. I plunged forward in a suicide attack.

"This has to do with the fire on Borwyn, doesn't it?" My
option for retreat disintegrated. It was all or nothing now.
"What's this company afraid of? Why is everything hidden?"

My eyes having adjusted to the darkness, I observed
the sparse decoration of the office. A few images of people

in old-fashioned football uniforms hung on the walls, and there were two bookcases filled with volumes. A clock and a few pieces of paper sat on Lexar's desk. I couldn't see any pictures that looked like Indy or family.

"You're a *cabeza dura*, aren't you?" Lexar answered. "You need to understand. There are a lot of things little people like you don't need to know."

That really irritated me. "What do you mean, little people like me? What don't I need to know? I know that somebody died in that Borwyn fire. It wasn't an accident." Then I stirred myself up for some unsupported bluster. "And I know that you know who had it burned."

"Huh. You don't know anything. Your kind has such feeble intellects. You can't fathom the complexities of this world. From time immemorial, the common people have needed elites to guide them. The national government has failed, so it's up to us, the special ones in local communities, to do that guiding. Don't even try to understand."

I took aim at what I thought to be his vulnerable heart. "Does that special elite include your daughter? What makes her so special?"

Apparently, I hit a vital organ. He jerked himself upright but didn't turn toward me. "Don't talk about my daughter!" he barked in a voice that was very near to yelling. "Don't even think about her. Don't ever see her again. Don't let me—soon, she'll be one of us anyway."

One of us? This was getting weird. "You and Indy are no better, nor worse, that anyone else," I said. "You've just got money."

"Get out. You don't know what you're talking about. Wealth means we're responsible for everything. You sheep have neither the wisdom nor the skills to run your own lives, but some of us have been prepared for leadership. You aren't. You're just getting in the way." He turned slowly toward me. Shadow darkened his face. "Get out! NOW! Or I'll call security and have you thrown out!"

"And leave your handheld. You don't own that, we do . . . and what's in it, as well."

I wasn't about to stand for that. "No, you don't. It belongs to me," I replied, and that was the truth. In fact, at that point, the device and its contents were about my most important possessions. As I turned to leave, I took it out, reached down and with a finger, deftly moved a few icons so that by the time I passed out of Lexar's office and into the light, I had transferred all my important files to my cloud storage and deleted them from my handheld.

A big guy wearing a black InfoNet Now knit shirt set upon me immediately. "Give it up," he said as he reached for my handheld, but I held firm.

"No, this belongs to me. You can check the serial number. You can't have it."

"Lemme check that and what's in it. Hold it up." I did, while he pressed his device against it for a few seconds. I wasn't surprised that when I pulled my handheld away, it was blank but for a blinking cursor.

"Hey! What the . . ."

"We took what's ours. You can rebuild it. You gonna leave peacefully, or do we throw you out?"

"I'll just go say goodbye to my friends, and I'll be out of here," I said. No sense waging a losing battle. With that, I departed from the splendid new InfoNet Now headquarters building, stepped out into the real world and then a block away, reentered the old InfoNet Now offices where I had been employed until a few minutes before. My unexpected appearance surprised Bowman.

"You aren't scheduled for today, are you?" he asked. "Something happening?"

"Yeah, I got fired. Curiosity killed this cat."

"What did I tell you? Didn't keep your head down far enough, did you," Bowman said.

"But you know there's a big story out there. Doesn't that just make you crazy?"

"Maybe you. But look what it did to you. Is it worth it? Now, what are you going to do?"

I had to admit that I hadn't really thought about that until he asked. And Bowman's down-to-earth wisdom hit me hard. "Hmm. Don't know. I just don't know," I replied. "Maybe I can get something freelancing."

We said our goodbyes, and as I went down the dark, old staircase one last time, I thought about my future. Another thunderstorm roiled the sky as I did some more thinking on the long commute on the train back to my little pad. I realized I would have to abandon it, along with pretty much everything else I owned. I faced the reality that where once I had lived in a nice apartment, now I likely would have to struggle to find someplace to live. Where once I had possessed the gadgets and toys of a comfortable life, now I could own only what I could carry. And where once I produced services of some value to society, now I'd have to find some way to restart a career in a field viewed by many as nothing more than a nuisance. Except that I realized I now held special knowledge that no one could take from me.

I had evidence that a major firm had killed an innocent person en route to taking property by questionable means. I fiddled with my handheld to rebuild its software, and then queried my cloud files. In an instant, all my important notes, and my sense of purpose, reappeared.

XII

My income, what little there was of it, now had evaporated. I pondered the decline of my material existence as I lay on my bed in my tiny flat that evening: from a comfortable high-rise apartment, to a tiny one-room flat, to who knows what. I had enough money for another week here and meals. I had to begin searching for a job immediately. I'd do whatever I could find, because the market for content providers was paltry, to say the least. My skills were not in demand: everyone thought they could communicate, so a hundred applicants lined up for every open content position when one appeared.

Income would be my immediate need. I had to sell what property I still owned, so I posted the availability of my goods and watched in the next few days as customers exchanged a few dollars for my little microwave, my refrigerator, my desk and chair, and finally my bed. I saved a few things I felt necessary to my mental survival: a couple print volumes of Shakespeare, Hemingway, Somerset Maugham, and my early edition of T.E. Lawrence's *Seven Pillars of Wisdom* that I kept for pride more than anything else. I set aside a couple pairs of pants, a couple shirts, some underwear, and an extra pair of decent shoes in a duffel bag and an old backpack. I slept on the floor.

My worldly goods proved to be worth enough to buy me a week's worth of housing and food, and to keep my hand-held functional for a while. I used that digital connection to search for a room that rented by the week and found a few possibilities in a distant suburban neighborhood. I didn't want to spend a lot on train fare, so I had to check out places within easy walking distance of one another.

I discovered lodging in a large old home that had been carved up into small living units many years ago. Similar homes in various states of disrepair filled a neighborhood where once laughing children played on green lawns. Attached garages at one time held big gas vans for those families, but now those garages had been converted to single-bed living quarters for people like me, the segment of society that paid by the week. Alongside some houses, crumbling old driveways still led away from the converted garages to curious sidewalks and streets that now rarely served their original purposes. Pedestrians occasionally used the broken concrete sidewalks that bordered the street, but weeds had sprouted in the cracks of the disintegrating street pavement where vehicles now rarely passed.

Carla Clogger, a small, round woman with frizzy, thinning gray hair, became my new landlord. She invited me into the foyer of her big house and opened a door to the immediate right, revealing a bright corner space of about a hundred square feet, with two tall windows facing the street and one to the side yard. "This was once the formal living room," the elderly lady said. "Goodness knows I don't need it, and I can use the income. Got four more roomers upstairs and one in the old garage. I live down the hall, in the back rooms of the house. My bedroom is on the other side of this wall." She patted an obviously altered side of the room.

"Rent is due by the week, in advance, please."

I pulled out my handheld and transferred the money to her account, because she didn't have her own handheld to accept the funds, and as I moved the money, I quickly calculated my stay in the comfortable room would be short-lived. But I slept well that night, and for the next few days, I used my handheld to find job openings and fill out applications. I interviewed for sales work at a high-end firm peddling handhelds, which were far out of my reach, and image-capturing devices that were even further beyond any budget I'd ever had. The bespectacled little fellow who queried me sounded positive, but in the end, he might as well have said "Don't call us, we'll call you," although he didn't. A day or so later, a financial firm invited me downtown for an "informational session." I thought it would involve public relations, but it turned out to be more like a marketing and sales position that wasn't in my skill set. Each experience, involving train fare and food, drained a little more of my wealth. I became more concerned each day.

The air grew chilly the first of the following week, but a couple positive factors lifted my spirits. Carla allowed me to use the last of my funds to pay for a few days lodging only, and then a temporary agency contacted me with a notice that I would be needed for work. The news heartened me, but the job turned out to be a test of endurance.

I joined a group of disheveled men very early the next morning in the cramped concrete-block offices of the temp agency. There, a leathery woman with short gray hair, a flannel shirt, and denim jeans gave us cards with an address and told us in a voice that sounded like rubber tires on gravel that we'd have to find our own way there. The ancient factory that matched those numbers sat amid a rail yard, and when the group had reassembled, we were led to a back loading dock brimming with innumerable stacks of square bags filled with a smelly lawn-care substance. The labeling warned that each bag held two cubic feet of product and weighed 20 pounds. Worse, the cold had frozen the contents and glued the squares together. An ancient foreman with a wool hat and a protrusive red nose ordered us to transfer all the square bags into empty rail boxcars that had been rolled up to the dock. He said a bot could have been programmed to do the work, but it couldn't be brought back to this obscure corner of the property, and besides, the company couldn't afford one. I was thankful for the income.

My hands froze first. The strenuous work exercised my body such that it warmed me, or kept me too occupied to notice the cold, but my nose soon equaled my hands in numbness. I was quite thankful at three in the afternoon when the foreman called off the work with about half the bundles transferred. Those who wanted could return the following day, he said, and when we reconvened the next morning, I noticed the group had shrunk by about half. But the sun soon broke through the clouds, warming the air and our spirits so that the work progressed more smoothly, if not more comfortably. At the end of the day, with the task complete, the company paid the crew in cash, probably because so few had bank accounts, I guessed. We weren't offered more work.

When I opened the door to the rooming house that evening, I encountered Carla waddling down the dark hall in her curious side-to-side limp. With the money in my hand, I paid for the rest of the week's lodging, but she declined to allow me to stay longer without rent in advance. At least she was helpful. "Why don't you try The Portal," she said. "I think the city runs it, or some agency. They have rooms, and you get fed." I thanked her and envisioned the end of my rope approaching.

A couple days later, I carefully folded my clothes into my duffel, stuffed my backpack with my few other possessions, and hit the road again. Without funds, I couldn't renew my handheld service, so I figured that my communication would have to be face-to-face for the foreseeable future. My more immediate goal was to find The Portal, so I could have a roof over my head. At the train stop nearest the rooming house neighborhood, I found a coffee shop where I could hook into the net for the price of a cup of java, and by the time I had reached the bottom of the bottomless cup, I had not only an address but a confirmed place to stay.

* * *

The Portal's location in an undesirable part of town scared me a little, and its gateway did not present a welcoming introduction for visitors. High fences topped with coils of razor wire bordered the walkway to the facility, indicating its proximity to the county prison. Indeed, The Portal appeared to be a converted portion of the jail, probably with origins as a minimum-security section. I didn't care. I was dog-tired by the time I stumbled through the front entrance doors, where a huge, friendly black man, with a space between his front teeth, greeted me as the desk clerk. I filled out some papers warning that I'd have to look for work during my stay there, and that my tenure was not unlimited and could be revoked at any time. In a few minutes, the large man led me to a small, spare, windowless dorm room with two plain beds, a night table between them, and little else. "Dinner will be served in the cafeteria at six p.m.," he said as he closed the door.

Before six, the aromas of prepared food led me to the dining area, a large multipurpose room with basketball back-boards on four sides. Men in all manner of dress and condi-tion packed dozens of foldable picnic tables. Women, I was told, stayed in a separate, undisclosed facility somewhere on the other side of town, and some of the men with whom I spoke expressed displeasure over that. Others understood: "They's worried we'll rough 'em up," one man said, "and I bet they're right." A few minutes before six, men started to assemble in a line in front of a set of double doors with windows looking into a kitchen. Uniformed guards came at six sharp to swing the doors open, revealing a cafeteria line with steaming plates of food already prepared by twisting, turning robots.

I felt hunger pangs as I shuffled down the line gather-ing food, but when I sat down at a table, I realized others were far hungrier than me. We had been offered a plate of pasta with a red sauce, some bread, a salad of assorted green vegetable matter, and a cup of water. One fellow at my table, dressed in denim and a dirty white T-shirt, lifted his plate and draggled his scruffy beard by literally pouring the pasta into his mouth. Others were more demure, but no less needy, scouring their plates clean with the plastic silverware.

The satisfying meal made evening in my dorm room more comfortable. My roommate the first night was a fellow named Dechen Wasgo who, like me, had lost a middle-class job and fairly comfortable income. This was his third overnight stay in The Portal.

"They'll let you alone for about a week," he said, "but after that you'll have to move on or move to The Pod. That's the multipurpose room that's converted into like a barracks, where you can sleep on cots, but you can't stay during the day, and you can't leave your belongings. There's thousands of men like us either waiting to get in here, or living out on the streets and not knowing this place exists. In about a week, it will be someone else's turn to come in here and clean up, and your turn to be out there wandering around."

That was incentive enough for me to look for work. For the next several mornings, I'd get up, shower, shave, enjoy the free cup of coffee offered in the cafeteria—they didn't serve breakfast—and take the train downtown to a library where I could pore over employment listings in the databases and take notes. Evenings began in the dining hall with meals mostly of pasta. Although one night, we had wraps filled with some kind of meat-like substance, a cheese food product, and greens. And then another night, a church group from a wealthy community pushed the robots aside and served us a meal highlighted by meatloaf made from what tasted like real ground beef, natural green beans, steamed potatoes, and chocolate cake for dessert. It was heavenly.

I dined with some strange characters those evenings. One fellow had lost a leg somehow, making it difficult for him to carry a plate through the food line, so I helped him to a table. I learned he was married, with a wife and triplet young sons in the women's shelter. "I miss 'em like crazy," he said. "I wish they'd let me in to see 'em, but I have to show I can support a family. So we get together during the day sometimes. I've just gotta find work."

I don't know if he did, because I never saw him again and never got his name. Another evening I met a man everyone called Taco, who claimed he had been one of the last broadcast radio producers "until the whole damn industry automated. Fake voices! Machine-written scripts. Nothing for humans to do." I shuddered to think how close that was to my experience.

It turned out Dechen was right about the limits of my stay in the dorm at The Portal. After about five days, the big clerk at the front desk stopped me on my way out.

"You can stay in the dorm room two more days, then you'll have to move to The Pod," he said politely.

"But it's a weekend," I replied. "It's hard to find work on the weekend." Yet, I knew the rules, and it was difficult to criticize their hospitality. Nevertheless, my funds for train fare had dwindled to almost nothing; I left the downtown library late that day, shrouded in desperation as a weather front swept through downtown, bringing a cold rain and wind. I had used up my train fare getting there, so I faced a miles-long hike back to The Portal.

It was getting dark when I found myself wandering through the city's ritzy restaurant district, an atmosphere of glitzy lights, glamorous clothes, and stern doormen that made it feel like I had entered an entirely different dimension. I recalled that once I had dined in these establishments with Indy and her friends. Now, with wet, cold feet, I sought a bit of shelter from the rain. I found it at a covered payment kiosk in the middle of a parking lot, surrounded by big shiny cars, mostly gas-powered exotic marques.

I stood there for a few minutes, trying to ward off the rain and cold, when a large white car with darkened windows drove up. It stopped next to me and a window rolled down slightly.

"Hey, son, do you operate that thing? We need to park," a male voice asked from inside.

I could feel dry heat pouring out of the window as I leaned forward into the cold rain. "I think it takes a cash card," I replied. I didn't know, really, but it seemed simple enough.

"Here. Make it work," the voice said, and a gloved hand and jacketed arm jutted out, looking and acting more like a glove on a broomstick than a human appendage. I took the card and waved it in front of a sensor, which spit out a code that directed the vehicle to a parking spot.

When I handed the card back, reality and desperation seized me. My list of options had shrunk to this. "Sir," I said, "could you spare some cash for train fare for me? I need it to get home."

"Geez," the voice said as the hand pulled in. I heard voices in the darkness inside the car. My wretchedness couldn't have been more profound, until the hand reached out again, holding paper money.

"Get a job," the voice said as I took the offering. The hand retracted again and the car pulled away. Thoroughly humiliated, I unfolded the bills and found substantially more than train fare back to The Portal. I felt thankful for the generosity as I looked around for the train stop.

When I found the train, I climbed aboard a mostly empty car. It lurched forward, and I plopped into a seat, dripping wet but thankful for the warm interior. I was even more grateful for the dry contrast of the dorm room, so it was with some remorse that I packed my belongings into my backpack in the morning in preparation for moving to The Pod. After each evening meal, diners who planned to stay at The Portal folded up the tables and rolled them to the side, making the multipurpose room a large open space. Then the dozens of would-be houseguests pulled plastic-and-fabric cots out of a storage area on the unused performance stage at one end of the room, set them up in reasonably neat rows, and stashed their goods under the cots as they prepared to sleep.

I endured this routine for several days. The stretched fabric of the typical cot made it uncomfortable, and I slept fitfully, growing more frustrated each evening as I weighed the alternative outdoors. Then one evening, while I enjoyed a rare interlude of sleep, someone made off with my decent pair of genuine leather shoes, which I had neglected to stuff in my backpack under my cot. I awoke to realize that I would have to use my pair of worn plastic shoes; the loss of my good shoes would hamper my mobility and make it more difficult to look reasonably presentable.

That morning, I stared into my cup of coffee and brooded over my circumstances. In my frustration, I reduced everything to simple terms: Paul Lexar had done this to me. He had punished me effectively, shut me up, and reduced me to one of the powerless little people he had described. In my mind, I returned to the big Borwyn Street event, the crackling blazes and the ashes drifting down like multicolored snow. I seriously doubted that my search for the truth about that fire had been worth the resulting afflictions.

My wrath was interrupted by the big desk clerk, who tapped me on the shoulder. "There's someone here to see you," he said. "Out in the lobby." Perhaps it was someone to offer me work, I thought, or maybe the thief who took my shoes, feeling remorse.

The lobby doors swung open to reveal Lucy Noble, tall and not especially well dressed in a baggy sweater and denim jeans, and her son, no longer as tubby as I remembered him. They stood at the reception desk, grinning broadly.

"You, uh, you're a hard person to find," Lucy said. "I've been all over town looking for you. I don't have a handheld, so I couldn't contact you. Where have you been?"

"I've been around," was all I could think of to say.

"Don't you know you're all over the social networks? Word's out that InfoNet Now canned you. We all know what that means, those heartless creeps. You're screwed. How long can you last? You got any money?"

"I figure till the end of this week, maybe next week," I lied. "It's nice here, but I can't stay forever. I'll have to move eventually."

"Then what? Got any ideas?"

"I haven't thought that far."

"Well, I have an idea." She leaned forward, grinning broadly. "I heard you broke up with Indy, so you can't expect any help from her. You're going to move in with me. At least till you get your feet on the ground."

"What? I can't expect—"

"You helped me when those jerks pulled the rug out from under me. It's the least we can do. I'm renting a little house. Not all that big, but there's only me, my new boyfriend, and Jamaal. The couch is plenty comfortable. That's what you're gonna do. Start getting ready. We'll help you get your stuff on the train."

I wasn't in a position to say no. I went back to my cot, grabbed my backpack with my books and my clothes, such as they were, so that in minutes, I was signing out and walking away with Lucy and her son. Within a few hours I had a new address.

Lucy lived with her boyfriend, Adam Khalid, and her son, now a gangly six-year-old, in a very old two-story house on the extreme outlying edge of a middle-level suburb. The place obviously had experienced many lives; years before, at its construction, it featured real wood banisters leading upstairs to two bedrooms. Oak-like framing around the house's many windows and doors looked pretty authentic, although ages of use had broken some corners to reveal the faux foam resin substance. Previous occupants had obscured most of the imperfections in the walls with coats of paint, but the nearly indestructible artificial-tile flooring so common in working-class homes had been retained. Lucy had added nice multicolored rugs in strategic locations, as well as a few pieces of colorful plastic furniture. The place had a living room, a rec room that families probably once used as a dining area, and a kitchen area that even included an old-fashioned oven and stove. When we arrived with my goods, Lucy pointed to a couch in the living room as my designated area. Clearly, her intention was to make my experience there homelike, if not sumptuous.

* * *

I experienced a whole new lifestyle in Lucy's home. Lucy's boyfriend, Adam, worked an evening shift running package sorters at a giant airport distribution center, so he came home well after midnight during the week. Some evenings, he and I stayed up late drinking beer and playing my handheld's bloatware video games that I could project on a wall. I learned that he drank too much and sometimes became disagreeable; another bad choice for Lucy, I decided, but none of my business. But as often as not, Adam was so tired after work that he could barely drag himself up to bed. Lucy worked as a clerk at the same place—that's where they had met—but her hours got her up and moving before the sun rose. She would drag Jamaal out of bed and send him off to a staging area for kids going to school later in the day. Sometimes, when they were in a hurry, Lucy even slapped together some pseudo-cheese on pieces of bread or mixed a nutrient shake for breakfast.

I worked at finding a job. I had saved a pair of nice synthetic-fiber pants, some cotton ones, and a couple decent shirts. Aside from my plastic shoes, I was able to make myself look reasonably presentable. However, I found there wasn't any demand for content providers, even when I told potential employers that I knew things about powerful people. They didn't seem to care or want to know.

Eventually, my skill at putting words together got me an adjunct job teaching basic writing at the area's community college. For the first couple weeks, I fibbed that I had a working digital connection, so I would have to race down to a library or coffee shop to create exercises and send them out to my vast herd of hundreds of unseen students. Then I'd get the exercises back and spend hours correcting and grading them manually, because the college couldn't afford the digital gizmos the state university used for that kind of work. Soon I got paid a little, more or less for piecework, so I could afford to renew my online presence.

Evenings were filled with an assortment of diversions. Lucy, a gregarious soul when times were good, often invited friends over from work. One evening, my old co-content provider Bowman visited, along with an overweight older woman named Maggie, who sat on my sofa wheezing as she rocked side to side, regaling us with sermons about politics and her declining health, in equal measure. "I have vision impairment, so I'm legally blind," she complained. "My legs and feet hurt so much I can't walk more than a few steps." She had tiny eyes set in a broad face with rosy cheeks, topped by a frizzy bird's nest of blond-and-gray hair. From that peak down to her bloated ankles, her appearance confirmed her miseries.

"You know, if I could afford it, I could get these things treated," she said. "Like digital optical replacements. Or fix it so I could walk. They have such good prostheses now that you never know what's real and what's not. Way beyond knee or hip replacements. Whole legs. Whole arms. All you gotta do is be able to pay for them."

"It's just aging," Bowman interjected. "Nobody beats Father Time."

She laughed, and we all chuckled. "No, it's the mess we're in now. You got a few people who can afford drugs and treatment to keep themselves alive, and there's the rest of us suffering souls."

She was edging into bombast, I thought, and I interrupted. I remembered what life had been like just a short time ago. "We survive pretty well here. We can eat. We have a roof over our heads, and a place to sleep. There's government schools for the kids."

"That's only survival," Maggie replied. "Have you seen the stats on declining life spans? Lord knows, I'm just hanging on. And lifestyles? There was a time when almost everybody who wanted one had an e-pod, or even a gas car. That was back when there was oil. Everyone had a big television monitor, and cheap access to programming. Some of it was even free broadcasting. Everybody had a handheld. Who can afford that now?"

I cringed and shrank into the coach where I was sitting, at the far end from where Maggie had positioned herself. I had worked hard to earn my handheld, I thought. Bowman must have had the same thing in mind. "Whoa. Some of us got those for work," he said.

"What happened?" I asked innocently.

"It takes money to make money," Maggie replied. "We all live payday to payday, if we get paid at all. Nobody has anything extra to set aside. Meanwhile, there are the few people who own things, who have money. They've propagated a myth over time that they're the ruling class, who deserve to be in charge because they've earned their wealth, and that there's everybody else: the workers. Truth is, most of those rich people got their wealth passed down to them.

"It's all legacy and connections," she continued. "They all serve on the same boards, belong to the same clubs, go to the same restaurants. They see to it that things fall their way, and they let out just enough of the wealth to keep us little people satisfied. Like building a school every now and then. Or building trains, but remember the trains run on roads that the e-pod people enjoy."

"Oh, come on," I blurted. "Maybe wealth bought some people a better education, and a way to make more money, but it's hardly a ruling class. They don't rule me. I can go wherever I want, and pretty much do what I want."

"Can you, really? Where are you living now?" Maggie asked.

"He's okay," Lucy interjected, and we all laughed. "So what can we do?"

I joined the movement. "Yeah. Do we get out the pitchforks and protest signs?"

Maggie shook her head and sighed. "I don't know. Once upon a time, votes counted for something, but since the federal government withered, all we have are local politicians. But they make sure the right people run for office. And even voting's been corrupted. Look how the system works. Where you're living, for example, the zoning board approves the plans of developers who are friends of the board, the developer pays for a building permit, the engineers on the job pay for a license to do the work, and the buyers pay a tax. What do you get for that? The zoning board decides who lives where and then favors some places but not others. Surely, some people are paid off, but you won't find out because the records are sealed."

I nodded. She was right about those records.

We moved on to other subjects of conversation, but that night, I wasn't comfortable, which wasn't unusual because I didn't sleep well on that sofa. The narrow plane where I tried to recline consisted of three cushions that felt like big sacks of rice, although I didn't complain because Lucy's largesse was keeping me off the streets, literally. And Maggie's jeremiad brought me back to the investigation that had gotten me into so much trouble. I pondered how to firmly link the Gheni girl's murder to the interlocking directorates that Maggie talked about and Proffitt had feared.

Zealots weren't the only people to visit Lucy's living room. Another guy, Ned Ludd, and his girlfriend told great stories of their adventures around the country on an old gas motorcycle. They had witnessed a brilliant meteor shower in Montana, hiked trails in Utah, and lived in a tent on the shores of a beautiful lake in upstate New York that once had been a fishing paradise until acid rain sterilized it. At least, those were the tales Ned told us. Unfortunately, excess beer often lubricated the evening such that the proceedings became unpredictable.

We didn't openly disagree with the fellow. Bearded, with long, wavy blond hair, he displayed muscled bulk that filled any doorway he passed through. His experiences included some years in the state penitentiary, where he had learned to use nunchucks that he loved to demonstrate. He would swing the two sticks connected by a chain in an intricate dance in front of us in the living room, while his skinny, bespectacled blond girlfriend gazed at him in awe. The rest of us avoided the sticks *whooshing* past us. It's a wonder Lucy's plastic furniture wasn't smashed to pieces.

"You know, these will protect you in almost any situation," he bragged as he upended a beer bottle and sucked down the contents. "I've got friends that, like, you wouldn't want to mess with. They know better than to fool with me."

I fooled with Ned, however. I found his stories fascinating, and he seemed innocuous enough, once you got past his threatening appearance. I teased him about his tough friends and what they, and he, had done to get put behind bars.

"They was, like, all kinds," he said. "There was one guy, real quiet, who was in for forgery and passing bad checks. Then, there was this other guy, he was, like, the opposite. Real badass dude. In for second-degree murder. Beat a guy to a pulp for messin' with his girlfriend." If Ned thought that guy was a threat, I couldn't imagine how rough the fellow must have been.

"Lotsa burglary, you know," he continued. "It was, like, every third one was a thief. Some of them were, like, so messed up on drugs that they couldn't get help or know how. So they'd be vagrants on the street, and take stuff to eat."

"Any really unusual cases, strange crimes or people?" I asked.

"Everybody in there is strange. This one guy, he, like, was a corrupt cop. Nicest guy to talk to, but he got caught stealing drug money from a dealer. The dealer complained to him and got beat up from the feet up. That went to court, and the cop wasn't able to articulate the facts in his own favor.

"I met a firebug, too. Not in prison, but in transition counseling here in town. Those were, like, strange groups. You just knew some of them were full of BS and ready to get back out on the streets again." Ned rose up and headed in the direction of the beer cooler.

I almost fell out of my chair leaning forward. "You know an arsonist? Somebody local?"

"Yeah, sure," Ned said when he returned to his chair. "I still got some acquaintances with, like, questionable jobs."

"You remember that big fire on Borwyn Street about two years ago?" I asked. "It was arson. You don't suppose your firebug friend was involved, do you?"

Ned said he didn't know, but I pursued the issue. How many arsonists could there be in a midsize city? "Could you, maybe, link me up with this guy?" I asked. "Just 'cause I want to talk. I don't need to know names, addresses, or any ID. I'm just interested in that particular fire."

"That's weird. You, like, got a thing for fires? Well, I say whatever floats your boat. I'll poke around for you. No promises, though."

"None expected. Thanks."

Ned went back to his nunchuck routine, and I sat back, far away from their menacing arcs, thinking about the kind of information I could get out of a real firebug. I wasn't interested in technique nor strategy to ensure a good conflagration and not get caught. I wanted to know who bankrolled the crime.

XIII

Ned was as good as his word. About a week after I requested an audience with an arsonist, I was sitting in Lucy's living room, grading bad student writing with my handheld projector and virtual keyboard. Thunder rumbled in the distance, and rain spattered the roof of the porch. Lucy answered a knock at the door; there was a brief conversation, and Lucy turned to me.

"Somebody wants to talk with you," she said in a matter-of-fact way.

I turned and confronted a presence that took my breath away. In the doorway stood a large woman, almost as big as Ned Ludd, with broad shoulders, an equally broad belly, and wide hips. She had short, blondish-gray hair, a couple small earrings, and tattoos down her neck. She wore a T-shirt, a dirty military jacket, and blue jeans.

What took me aback, though, wasn't her casual fashion sense as much as her visage. I had never seen a look that projected such malevolence. Her cold steel-gray eyes bespoke a menace enhanced by her dark brows and small, tight lips. And when she spoke her voice amplified the feeling.

"Ned Ludd told me to come here."

"Uh, really? When?" There was an enormous flash of lightning, and almost immediately, a crack of thunder shook the house.

"He said you were maybe interested in me doing a job. You gonna invite me in? It's storming out here."

Classic horror tales came to mind. The vampire couldn't enter your home unless invited. But I stepped aside to let her in.

"What kind of job are you thinking?" I asked.

"He said you like fires."

"Uh, oh, yeah, yeah." Frightening things started to come together. "You know about that kind of stuff, huh? Here, sit down. Let's talk."

She plopped herself down on one of Lucy's plastic chairs and set the big purse she carried on the floor at her feet. "I can do anything, for the right money. Wadda you want?"

"Well, really what I want is information about fires that already happened."

"You a cop?" She curled up her nose; her evil gray eyes got even darker, and she sneered. "I'm outta here."

"No, no, no. Don't. You know Ned would never send you here if he couldn't trust me. Trust me."

"Why?"

"I'm just a poor unemployed content provider. I'm trying to do a story on a fire in town that a friend told me wasn't, um, an accident. I thought you might know about that end of the business."

"Mehbe. What's it worth to ya?"

Here, I ran into a wall. I wasn't financially prepared for this, and I wasn't about to give her my account numbers.

Then I remembered that months before, when Lucy and her son were living in my place, the grocery had forced me to use cash. I still had a little of that somewhere among my belongings. And when I was down and out, the people in the car gave me cash. I offered the woman 100 dollars, and her dark eyes opened. I rummaged through my packs, found the paper money, and displayed it.

"What fire?" she asked, and when I said 112 Borwyn Street, she straightened up from slouching in her chair, almost like she was proud to accept the recognition.

"I'm the best. People know they can come to me to get the job done good. Usually, nobody even knows the fire wasn't an accident.

"That one was different. They wanted me to pull out all these paper files and use them to start the burnin'. Real particular like. Lots of old papers, and old disks that didn't burn worth shit, just melted. And they even got the gasoline to soak the stuff."

I was getting breathless, and my eyes must have been as big as plates. "They? Who's this 'they'? And how did you arrange this, uh, transaction?"

"A guy dressed real nice walked up to me on the street one day, handed me an envelope, and walked away without a word. A note in the envelope said if I wanted to make some money, I should be at 112 Borwyn Street that night at nine.

"I thought okay, so I showed up there at nine, and in a few minutes this big guy in a knit shirt walks up to me and says, 'What do you think of this building here?' I says, 'I don't really care one way or another,' and the guy says his employer doesn't like it and wants it down, and they think I could help them. I says, 'I'm no contractor,' and he says, 'We hear you're good at demolition,' so we went and had a cup of coffee, and he's hinting that they're lookin' for someone who knew about accidents that burn places. I was gettin' suspicious, but I says that a job like that would cost a lot of money.

"He says, 'We can afford it,' and pulls out a huge wad of real cash money. He starts calling me his 'contractor' and says if they're going to hire me, I had to start the 'decon-struction,' he called it, in particular rooms on the first and second floors, and I had to be sure the files burned. Then he counts out twenty-five thousand dollars in cash and says I'll get the other half when the job is completed. They know where I live, he says, and they'd deliver it. Before he walked out, he told me the next night after dark, I'd find a big can of gasoline in the alley behind the building.

"Sure 'nuff, it was there, so I knew what we were talking about."

"Okay, how am I supposed to believe all this?" I asked. "Paper money? Are you just giving me a line of bullshit? I want proof if I'm going to give you this," and I waved the old 100 dollars in paper money in the air. Outside, lightning flashed, followed closely by a roll of thunder.

"The building's down, isn't it?"

"Did you get the rest of the money?"

"Yep, sort of. A few days after the fire, this cute young thing dressed in a business suit appeared at my door. Couldn't have been more than twenty-one. Fake blonde. Nice shoes with heels. She hands me this envelope real quick and starts to walk away, but I grabbed her and pulled her in. She was scared to death.

"I opened the envelope and counted out fifteen-k bills. I told her she was tryin' to cheat me, but she's whining that she was just told to deliver it, and that she didn't know nothin'. So I cuffed her about the head and shoulders, and she's crying and wiggling, and all she says is she doesn't know nothin'.

"I says, 'Who sent you?' more than once, and swatted her a few more times, and she's crying and all she says is, 'My boss, my boss.' 'Okay,' I says, 'you go tell your boss to get the rest of my money, I'll be following you' and she runs out. By this time, her lip was bleeding, and I may have busted one of her teeth. I thought about following her, but I wasn't as fast as she was, even in her heels. 'Course she didn't come back, and I never did get that money.

"There. I told you what I know. Now you owe me some money. Gimme the cash now."

It hurt to pass my 100 dollars to her, but she had given me lots of new information. She grabbed the bills and said if she found out I squealed on her, I would be "one sorry ass." Then she quickly rose and stepped toward the door. My mind was spinning so that I couldn't think of more questions to keep her there, or even if I wanted to keep her around. So I let her walk. "Thanks for helping me out," was all I said as she stepped out into the dark, rainy night, but she didn't say a word. It occurred to me that I hadn't even asked her name, or whether she knew, or cared, about Chanya Gheni's death. I doubted that she would answer to either.

I dropped onto my couch-bed as my mind churned with more questions than I had before this mystery woman appeared. Who had hired her? That one was easy: Lexar and his boards—the university trustees and the city council—wanted the building down. But how could I make the connection? And why the emphasis on the files? What was in them?

Lucy returned to her living room. "*Ick*. Who was *that?* What did she want with you? I don't think you should meet her here again. Find some alley or something."

My internal compass was spinning, seeking direction. I didn't know what to do. "I owed her some money," I said.

XIV

A couple days later, my handheld stopped working. That put me incommunicado, a real pain. Since most of the great mass of society couldn't afford a handheld and all its utility, I always felt fortunate that I owned one and could set aside enough money to pay for its services. I had needed it for my work, and now I needed the connection for my teaching job and, more important, to search through records.

The first problem I had to solve was continued income. I had to figure out how to grade the written work submitted by my students and send notes to them. I revisited the old ways I had used when I originally got the job: I corresponded via the local library connect center, where I waited in line for an hour to get on to an ancient tablet with no keyboard and no projection. I handwrote notes on the student papers with a stylus, then bought enough mail time to transmit the graded work back to them. I might as well have used an ink pen and paper. It was inconvenient and expensive, to say the least.

The morning after my handheld failed, I took the train down to my handheld's consumer center, which was, of course, a subsidiary of InfoNet Now. There, I waited in line patiently for half the morning until a customer service rep took my device and examined my account.

"Hmmm. Everything seems to be in order," he said as he fired it up, then flipped it over and popped open the back. "It works fine. Don't know what's going on. I'll have to go deeper into the system to see why you can't get service. Could be upgraded, though.

"Meanwhile, you're paid up. We'll get things working and get back to you as soon as possible. Would you care to upgrade to a higher-level device? We have a promotion going on."

I said no to that, after being assured I would be back online in a week or so. For a while I would be without a handheld, so I'd have to live like the majority of the population. I returned to Lucy's that evening in time to encounter her just stepping out.

"I left you a note," she said. "Two goons stopped by today to visit me. Two big women. I'm sure they were from InfoNet Now. They told me I'd better get rid of my houseguest, or they'd have the bank end my lease."

"What did you do?" I asked, while I envisioned a return to life on the street.

"I told them to go to hell. I said I had a legal lease, and I could invite as many guests as I want. They told me I better watch out or I'd be homeless. I said InfoNet Now already had done that to me, and there wasn't much more they could do legally to try to ruin my life."

"Thanks, Lucy. You're a real friend. I don't know how to thank you."

"They don't scare me. By the way, be sure to be here this evening. Don't go anywhere. See you later."

I didn't see her son, so I knew I wasn't babysitting. Nevertheless, being voluntarily imprisoned, I couldn't go out for dinner, so I was stuck with scraps of bread and peanut butter. After that satisfying meal, I sat and burrowed into the pages of T.E. Lawrence's *Seven Pillars of Wisdom*, until about midevening when I heard a knock at the door. A shrill bolt of fear flew down my spine as I anticipated another visit from the arsonist. I gripped the heavy book to defend myself.

But I dropped it when I opened the door. There in front of me stood Indy, her dark hair, backlit by the porch light, seemingly rimmed in gold. Slimmer than I remembered, she wore a loose white button-down blouse, jeans, and worn leather moccasins I had seen her wear around her apartment.

"You're a hard person to find," she said.

"Uh, I'm off-line. Out of touch with everybody. My handheld was shut down for some reason," I stammered.

"I had to contact Lucy at her work to get your address. Boy, was I surprised. She's saved your ass, huh?"

"For the time being. C'mon in. What brings you here?"

"My Alfa e-pod. No, really, I gotta talk with you. I'm serious. I'm in a mess."

I was beginning to melt. I drew breath only with difficulty. What was going on here? "Sit down. We don't have much here, but can I get you something? Water? Maybe I can find some pretzels or something. What's up?"

She glided over to my couch and looked up at me with open, pleading eyes. "No, thanks. I just need your advice. It's my father. He and his people are really harassing me. It's this 'family legacy' thing. You know what he's like."

"Wow. Yeah, I know what he's like, but don't really know him," I said. In my mind, I debated telling her what

I really had discovered about her father. "I know he's, um, pretty ruthless. He's used to getting his way."

"Amen. Now he sends me notes telling me that because of this health thing I'm going to be out of commission for a few months. Months! What the hell is going on? I feel fine, okay, maybe a little weird at times, but he says there's no option."

"You're an adult. Say no. Surely there are other options. Maybe I can help you."

"I really appreciate that." Indy visibly softened as the tension seemed to evaporate. "I thought you'd understand. I don't have other people to talk to. The people I know through my father just say I'm lucky to get this attention. It's like they're in their own bubble. The world outside it doesn't affect them. They just don't see any other way of life."

I touched her hand, feeling its softness. She curled her fingers around mine and squeezed gently. She must have seen the yearning in my eyes. "Don't get me wrong," she said quietly. "You and I can't go down the same path again. You're not like me. I like people. You're just an observer. You watch things, but you don't get involved. You have no heart."

"Hey, like I told you, I'm a content provider. I look for content. But you pull feelings out of me. I care about you. All this worries me. Do you have any idea what they're treating you for?"

"They took me in again, for an 'outpatient procedure,' they said. Look at what they did." She pulled her blouse down away from the back of her neck, and I found little pink scars that began at the port on her neck and ran in a parallel course down either side of her spine. A few inches down, the lines converged at a small plastic square—not a medical port but a tiny electronic component. Even in the dim light I could see it was an interface of some kind.

"What are they *doing* to you?" I blurted. "Are you being hooked up to some kind of machine?"

"It's supposed to help my walking in the future. I didn't know I had trouble. It hurt like hell when they did it."

"This has got to stop until you get some answers. I'll help you get to the bottom of this."

"Thanks, but I'm a big girl. I can handle myself. It's my own father, after all."

"I don't think you realize what you're dealing with. I found out your father won't stop at anything, and I mean anything. He . . . he . . . let's just say he thinks he's above the law."

"There you go again. Bring me proof and maybe I'll believe it."

"I've got evidence." Then something connected in my mind. Indy worked in InfoNet Now as a payroll accountant. She had access to all kinds of employee records. I couldn't hope to get into InfoNet Now, being persona non grata there.

"You could help me help you," I continued. "I know of a woman at InfoNet Now who had some medical issues like yours a while back, but I don't know her name. If I could find her, maybe I could . . ." I was only stretching the truth a little bit. "Could you dig into the records and see what women took a day or two off about this time a couple years ago? I'll get the exact dates."

"I could. What's this for?"

"It might be related to your experience. Get me names, and I'll find out." My need to know was dragging me into a tangled web. I had to change the subject to keep from sounding suspicious.

"The problem now is you. We've got to stop your father and his friends from hurting you."

"Okay. Like I said, I appreciate your offer, but I think I can deal with my father myself. I just need someone to talk to. I know where you are now. I would like to know what this medical stuff is. I'll see about those records." She rose from the couch without apparent discomfort, turned, and opened the door.

"And I'll take care of that handheld for you. See you soon."

I took a deep breath as I watched her walk out into the darkness. The door of her e-pod parked at the curb flipped up. She gave a little wave and climbed in without seeing my return gesture, which I continued long after the car whirred away down the street.

XV

I don't know how she did it, but Indy kept her promise. Midmorning the next day, my handheld awoke with a buzz as advertising, student papers, and all kinds of information rolled in. Thus reconnected with the outside world, I sat down to read and evaluate bad college writing. I dropped that homework like a sales pitch on my handheld, though, when the device buzzed and showed me absentee files for three women who took medical days off from their InfoNet Now jobs just after the Borwyn fire.

I figured the girl who delivered the loot to the arsonist wouldn't have known what she was being sent to do. She wouldn't have understood why she was getting a bloody nose and a busted tooth, and she would have been terrified. Would she have gone first to the police or to the supervisor who sent her? Now, a couple years later, she probably wouldn't volunteer to renew the experience with just anyone. I'd have to come up with a fiction.

I used my handheld's video connection to call the names on the files. The first to answer was an older, gray-haired woman, so I begged off as a wrong number. The next was a plump, middle-aged woman with short, dark hair. Unless she had been binging on doughnuts since the fire, this wasn't the right one, either. The last number was a relatively new hire in the legal department named Judy Jabbora. A young blonde answered and confirmed her name.

"I represent a firm looking into InfoNet Now's employee healthcare plan, and we understand you had to take some time off as a result of a physical altercation associated with your job a couple years ago," I lied.

"Yeah, that was back when I was an intern," Judy said. "I was told the president's office would handle everything. I'll transfer you to them."

"No, thanks," I replied, but before I could hang up a male face popped up on the screen. "Mr. Lexar's office," the face said. It was the guy in the knit shirt who had emptied my handheld. I shut down quickly, but my electronic breadcrumbs had been spilled. On one hand, I had connected Lexar's office to the payoff. On the other, Lexar's office now knew what I knew. I slept with one eye open that night, and when I awoke in the morning from my fitful sleep, I resolved to stay indoors for a while.

Late in the afternoon that day, extraordinarily good news arrived on the handheld. A tiny firm that called itself Your Community Reporter, with whom I had corresponded during my tenure at InfoNet Now, as well as afterward, sent a message offering me a position: "We reviewed your documents and we're pleased with your work, especially your ongoing investigation into the Borwyn fire. However, we're disappointed that you describe yourself as a content provider. We don't call ourselves content providers. We're reporters, and if you're willing to be a serious journalist, we're willing to take you on."

They offered next to nothing in income, just pay by the story, but the opportunity sounded like opening the gates of heaven to me. Finally, someone appreciated my pursuit of the fire story and all its tentacles. They wanted me to begin Monday of the following week.

I rejoiced at the news. It deserved a celebration, but I realized there was hardly anything I could do in Lucy's spare household. I scratched around and found only some bread, a can of processed fake lunchmeat in the little refrigerator, a bar of government-processed cheese food, and an old beer that Ned had left behind one evening. I popped open the beer.

I sipped it with gleeful satisfaction and had just settled onto my couch-bed to savor the moment when my handheld buzzed again. I opened it to the image of Indy, sitting in her condo living room framed by the huge windows and the backdrop of the city. "Hey, guess what!" I blurted. "I've been offered a job as a real reporter!"

"I need you," she said. Without giving the slightest hint of recognizing my end of the communication, she continued, "Come over here as soon as you can. Please." She sounded agitated and unusually helpless.

"Sure. What's up?"

"Just get here as fast as you can."

That popped my bubble of joy, but her distressed tone sounded serious. So I finished my beer, cleaned up, slipped into the most decent clothes I could unroll, and considered my strategy. I could relay the information I had learned in my calls to InfoNet Now, in order to force Indy to recognize the reality of her father's guilt. I reconsidered; that was pretty dramatic and probably not an appropriate thing to do, since I had lied to her to get the contacts. Instead, I just hoofed it to the closest train platform, serenaded by thunder rumbling out of a dark and threatening sky. When I caught the next train into town, it was raining, and for 20 minutes or so, I looked out over a wet cityscape while I rehearsed what I likely would have to say.

Night had risen by the time I arrived at the stop across from Indy's big condo building. Bright lighting in its foyer reflected off the concrete at the entrance, highlighting the glass front doors. I splashed through puddles to the door and used my fingerprints to announce myself to the security system near the elevator, which to my surprise, opened quickly.

The glass-enclosed elevator *whooshed* me to the 30th floor and slid open to the little hallway in front of Indy's front door. I was about to touch the security unit there to see if it that, too, would recognize my fingerprints, but I held back my hand when I overheard a curious sound.

It was a voice I recognized. Within a second, I knew it was Indy's father, who had spoken to me only once, when he fired me. He sounded as agitated now as he did then. Briefly, I feared the spider had lured me into her web. Then I listened more closely.

"Indira, you don't have a choice," Lexar said in a tone that sounded like a command. "You're a child of wealth. This is your legacy."

"Don't give me that 'legacy' bullshit," Indy replied. "You don't own me."

"It's our destiny and our responsibility," Lexar said. "There are just a few of us special ones. Now you'll be one of us."

"What makes us so special? What makes *you* special?"

"Look out that window. Look at all those people. What have they got? Nothing. Now look at us. We've accumulated wealth. We're able to afford a better life. Now you'll have that better life."

Outside the front door, I decided to wait and listen to Indy's answer. She sounded defiant.

"What kind of better life? I like things the way they are now, except for your meddling."

"This isn't meddling. It's your future. I'm offering you more than you can imagine. You saw those family videos. I want you to continue that."

"Yeah, about those pictures. How old are some of those?"

"Let's just say I'm older than you think. Generations older. Our, um, social and financial status has bought me time. Extended my life."

"Sure, better medical care. Your care is making me feel miserable."

"Only for a time, I assure you. Let me handle everything and in a few short months, you'll be a different person, almost literally."

"You can't have my body."

"You'll have a better one."

"What? What are you talking about?"

"We have a, er, technique that has been applied to the few chosen ones of us. Only the tiniest of the top percent of society. We've gotten the benefits of the best research, the best procedures, the best care. It's expensive. Very expensive. It's been perfected in our labs, brought forward from old Soviet research. They probably got it from the Nazis. Now this science has helped me and a few other people extend our lives and keep our places in the world."

"And you want me to be your lab rat?" Indy interrupted. Her voice expressed dread.

"Oh, it's no experiment. I'll call my associates now, and they'll take you to our clinic. Then we'll prepare you . . ."

At that, I thought I better move in. But I wanted to hear more from him, thinking he might expose his guilt in his ranting. I recalled Indy's pride in having space for a live-in housekeeper who could have private access, a back door, so I slid silently to the end of the hall, found it, and tried my fingerprint on its security box. Sure enough, the old-fashioned lock clicked open, and I pushed the door in slightly, stepped into a darkened hallway, peered ahead, and saw Lexar with his back turned to me, lit by overhead lights in a chiaroscuro effect against the dark beyond in the living room as he continued his lecture. Outside, I could hear rain, lashed by a strong wind, pounding against the big windows.

"Look at me," he said. "I can still move like anyone, and I'm an early version."

"Early version?" Indy cried. "Version of what? Oh my God! You're not human anymore!"

"That's not true. I've just been, um, well, improved, and you will be, too. Molière said the body is a machine. Let's say we took that to its practical ends."

"But you're talking to me. I can see your face. It's you. Are you run by artificial intelligence or something?"

"No, no. I think on my own, although I'm connected to all the others. It's the same me from the neck up. You get to keep your voice. And your spine, if you want to be metaphorical. It's still my face, my brain, my mind. The rest below my head is just, well, enhanced. It won't wear out. And the knowledge—I've already got the experience of many, many years behind me. That's given me so much more wisdom than I could ever have gotten in a normal lifetime."

"No, no!" Indy blurted. "Like hell you're doing that to me!"

I stepped forward into the light, so that only a dinner table and chairs separated me from Lexar. I could see now his enormous size, compared to Indy and me. His golf shirt strained to contain his muscular-looking body, and he stood a good head above me.

"If you're so smart, how come you gave money to an arsonist," I announced. "That's pretty stupid."

Lexar spun halfway around, though not quickly. "What? What are you doing here? This is none of your business."

"John! Thank God you finally made it here!" Indy cried out from the dark living room behind Lexar.

"I think what you're doing to Indy makes it my business," I said. "And I think she needs to know how evil you are. Indy, I have solid proof now that your father ordered that building on Borwyn Street burned down. And somebody died in that fire."

"You insolent little swine."

"No, that's the writing machine you made us use. And I guess you mean Lucy Noble, too. Where do you get off threatening her, just because I live in her place? What gives you the right to take away the place where people live?"

"I don't threaten. I'm on the bank's board of directors. We decide for the good of the bank. We don't deal with riffraff like you, or people you associate with.

"Anyway, what makes you think you know what you're talking about?"

"I heard about some of it from a guy named Proffitt. You knew him. You probably eliminated him, too. And I talked to the arsonist you hired. I know everything, and I'm going to talk. Soon the government will know about you. The state attorney general. The governor."

"I own the governor."

"Doesn't matter. I'll go to those little people you don't think much of. I'm going to publish it all. I'm a reporter now, not a damn content provider."

"Oh, yeah?"

"Yeah. I've got sources in a straight line from your office door to cash in an envelope handed over to your firebug. I know you stiffed her ten thousand dollars. I bet your DNA is all over that wad of bills and the envelope it was delivered in. I even know the special instructions about files and things you wanted used to set the fire."

Lexar seemed to ponder what I had said for a second. Then he laughed heartily. "That was money well spent. I killed two birds with one stone, so to speak. I burned down a building in the way of the new place we're leasing to the state university so we can squeeze more money out of them, those fools. And I eliminated all the old research notes and records for our medical techniques. After we change over Indira, there won't be any more like us. We'll be unique. We'll be powerful. Meanwhile, you and the rest of the world will live your puny little lives of what, seventy years?

"And you won't get any DNA from these hands, son."

Lexar reached down and tossed the heavy table and a couple chairs aside as though they were flimsy cardboard. With his arms extended, fingers grasping, he lurched toward me so that I realized his bulk and height towering over me. In an instant, his hands closed around my neck. These were no fingers. They felt like mechanical devices. They squeezed incrementally, compressing my throat, blocking my breath. I was terrified.

"You don't want to kill me."

"Yes, I do. You're getting in the way, just like Indira's mother did."

I thrashed helplessly as my feet grew lighter and lifted off the floor. He shook me like a rag doll. I was gasping, seeing flashes of twinkling light. "You're worthless scum," he muttered.

Then, I caught a glimpse of Indy in the background behind Lexar, running toward her father with eyes wide and teeth gritted. She held her beloved tennis racket. She lifted it and, in a mighty two-handed forehand, swung and struck him with the edge of the racket square against the nape of his neck at the base of his skull, splintering the composite frame with a loud crack.

He dropped me instantly, and I fell in a heap on the floor, my legs limp as cooked noodles. As I fell, I saw Lexar spin faster than I thought possible, his right arm extended. It hit Indy's chest with a sickening, crunching *thump*. Then, he fell, stiff as a tree trunk with his limb still extended, hitting the floor with an impact that shook the building.

Indy meanwhile took several steps backward and fell to the carpet in a sitting position against a sofa. I crawled over Lexar's stiff body, sensing an electric-ozone aroma as I inhaled and exhaled painfully a few times to confirm that I still lived. I met Indy there on the floor and looked straight into her eyes. "You saved me," was all I could think to say.

She was gasping and wheezing. "No more like him," she said softly. Then she raised her arms and drew me toward her, sending a little shiver of concern through my mind.

But she lifted her head and kissed me. Heartache and tender longing passed out of her with a passion we had never shared before. When she finally pulled away, I tasted blood on my lips.

"I love you," she said. "Now, get out." Her breath escaped with the sound of a slow leak in a balloon.

"I can't leave you," I whispered. "You're in bad shape. I'll take you somewhere."

"You can't . . . You're guilty as hell. Those goons . . . will be here soon for sure . . . Now get out . . . I mean it."

"I didn't do anything."

"It's you and me. Who do you think . . . is going to be called guilty . . .? Go!"

"I won't. I can't. They'll take you and make you into something like him." I pointed at her father's stiff body, where I swear I saw a wisp of smoke rising from his neck. Then I reached for her, but her arms weakly pushed my hands away.

"Don't touch me. Let me be . . . I can . . . take care of myself. I'm probably . . . so damaged I'm . . . not worth saving anyway." She tried a weak smile. "Now get out . . .

I mean it . . . Go . . . Go . . . Don't make me . . ." She was wheezing seriously now.

I lifted myself up, looked down at Indy, and slowly stepped backward. "I can . . . Let me go get help."

"No! Get OUT!"

So I slid the door open, stepped across the hall, and into the glass elevator. Indy's door closed before I could look back at her.

By the time I stepped out into the night air, the rain had stopped and the skies were beginning to clear. As I walked across the street, I saw a few stars bright enough to burn through the perpetual city glow. A train pulled up, and I hustled to get in just before its doors slid shut.

XVI

So now, I'm sitting in this moving train pondering the situation. How could I leave Indy like that? She's right: I have no heart. My obsession with that fire story has robbed me of human feelings. I've become a detached observer, without compassion, just like she said.

It's time to face up to the truth. I've got to do something, even if Indy told me in no uncertain terms to get away.

The train is creaking to a stop. "Next stop . . . University Place," the train's speaker announces. The glittering new university tower at the stop reminds me that it rose up from a corrupt foundation that eliminated living human beings, and Indy's about to become another victim. When they find her, surely those ghouls will turn her into one of their kind.

I've been so sanguine about life. Things have always worked out. It's time to step up, do something real, get beyond my own selfish world.

I jump up and slip out of the train's sliding doors. If I hurry, I can make it back to Indy's place in no time.

I've got to run faster. I can hear my heart pounding: *da tump . . . da tump . . . da tump . . .*

Acknowledgments

I owe recognition and gratitude to a great number of people who provided expertise and hours of their time in the preparation of this work. Foremost in this multitude is Eunice Tiptree of Orwell, Ohio, an internationally known writer and great editor. Without her guidance on structure, content, and wording, this book would be incoherent babble. In addition, I thank the Rev. Dr. Jack Smith of Deming, New Mexico, for ideas in the process of building this story and use of direct language. I owe Fred Marion of Kettering, Ohio, thanks for moral support and insight on the writing life. Terry L. Lucas Jr., retired police officer and storyteller extraordinaire, supplied special content and advice. Seasoned travelers Kathleen Palahniuk and Theresa Avila-John supplied unique perspectives about technology and interpersonal communication in the future.

Last, I owe my greatest thanks to my wife, Karin Avila-John. No fan of science fiction, she nevertheless offered patient support through the writing, editing, and production of this book. Her love provides the model for my characters in this work.

www.ingramcontent.com/pod-product-compliance
Lightning Source LLC
Chambersburg PA
CBHW051924240626
47153CB00004B/1360